ASTR

Mikael Niemi wa[...]
Pajala, Sweden and [...]
for adults, *Popular Music*, was awarded the
August Prize and was made into a film in 2004.
It has sold over a million copies worldwide and
has been translated into thirty languages. Among
his published books are two collections of poetry
– *Näsblod under högmässan* (Nosebleed during
Morning Service) (1998) and *Änglar med
mausergevär* (Angels with Mausers) (1989) – and
a young adult novel, *Kyrkdjävulen* (The Church
Devil) (1994).

MIKAEL NIEMI

Astrotruckers

TRANSLATED FROM THE SWEDISH BY
Laurie Thompson

VINTAGE BOOKS
London

Published by Vintage 2008

2 4 6 8 10 9 7 5 3 1

Copyright © Mikael Niemi 2004
English translation copyright © Laurie Thompson 2007

First published with the title *Svålhålet* by Norstedts Förlag AB,
Stockholm in 2004
First published in Great Britain by Harvill Secker in 2007

Vintage
Random House, 20 Vauxhall Bridge Road,
London SW1V 2SA

www.vintage-books.co.uk

Addresses for companies within The Random House Group Limited
can be found at: www.randomhouse.co.uk/offices.htm

The Random House Group Limited Reg. No. 954009

A CIP catalogue record for this book
is available from the British Library

ISBN 9780099490722

The Random House Group Limited supports The Forest Stewardship
Council (FSC), the leading international forest certification
organisation. All our titles that are printed on Greenpeace approved
FSC certified paper carry the FSC logo. Our paper procurement
policy can be found at www.rbooks.co.uk/environment

Printed and bound in Great Britain by
CPI Cox & Wyman, Reading RG1 8EX

Contents

Farewell to the Liviöjoki

The narrator takes a sauna by the Liviöjoki and bids farewell, for now, to Tornedalen

The sun hung low over the tree-clad horizon to the north. Its quivering red disc was reflected in the water and split into long, red brush-strokes drifting on the fast-flowing surface. I sat on the riverbank and let my melancholy drain away. The air was heavy with the smell of mud and July greenery. It was a quarter past midnight, totally calm, no wind, no movement in the leaves of the alder bushes. Only the mighty rush of the river. Thousands of tons of water picking their way through vast expanses of forest, a spine of water stretching into eternity. You could watch it for ever. The river constantly changing but always the same, even so. Just like the fire. The man-made campfire. Millions of years of comradeship.

I raked together the smouldering branches, watched flames leaping up. The embers glowed bright red and sharp among the ashes. Thin, white smoke rose, almost transparent, floated slowly upstream, a ghostly spectre wriggling over the surface of the water, dipped suddenly down, rose up again and then vanished. Hanging low over the fire was a grayling, speared on a newly whittled green sapling. Its skin sizzled in the glowing heat, and I carefully rotated the spit. The grayling had taken a Westrin fly near the spot where a little beck flows into the river, darted back and forth with thrusts of its big dorsal fin, and I had felt touched once again by life. Life, close at hand. Now the fish was being slowly grilled, a delicacy weighing around half a kilo. The old rod I had fished with as a boy was leaning against a deformed birch tree, its trunk bearing witness to a violent rush of thawing ice. The fish's head and guts were scattered on the riverbank, small silvery scales glittering in the sun.

I tugged gently at the dorsal fin. It came loose, the fish was ready. I sat down by the fire and started eating with my fingers. Pulled the white flesh from the pin-thin bones and filled my mouth with it. It was like eating warm snow. A gentle caress of the palate, a wisp of smoke. River and fire. I closed my eyes to preserve the memory. Knotted it into my tender heart.

Feeling satisfied and serene I strolled out onto the

floating jetty. The planks rocked under my weight, the water clucked and squelched. I was walking on water. Walking on the river's skin, it was flowing directly underneath my feet. The sauna was built on a raft and anchored with chains. Wooden boards nailed together, a little timber cabin bobbing up and down on the water.

The heat struck me as I entered the changing room. Full of expectancy I undressed and hung my clothes on the hooks. Then I opened a beer and drank the first frothy swig. Tasted the malt, felt the cold prickling in my throat. Last of all I opened the door of the sauna itself. The heat was intense and resinous. I used a stick to open the red-hot door of the fire box, pushed in some pieces of wood and climbed up onto the highest bench. The copper ladle was gleaming in the pail. I grasped the smooth, worn wooden handle and filled the scoop, held it up for a brief moment and watched the river water trickling over the rim.

Then I poured. The water swirled down through the air, smacked into the stone box and was transformed into scratching, biting steam. I poured again and felt my ear lobes burning, leaned forward awkwardly and breathed in through my fists. My fingers still smelled of fish. And I felt such bliss. Such fervent, vulnerable bliss.

Tornedalen.

It would exist for ever. I would carry it with me down the light years.

The roar of a jet suddenly explodes towards me from the direction of Mommankangas. Something black and heavy swishes through the stillness, it sounds like a P-42, from the emergency services. My last night, I think. My last night on Earth.

Steaming hot, I step out onto the platform. Stand there with the midnight sun in my eyes, and brace my naked foot against the wooden boards. Then I launch myself, headfirst, shoulders square. Sail through the air.

At full stretch I approach the surface of the river. My index finger grazes the film of water with the extreme tip of its nail. The water sags but holds firm, gleaming and tense. My reflection rises up from the depths. A twin, filled with darkness. It is the river staring me in the face, pressing the tip of its finger against mine.

Soon I shall be drenched, in a split second.

But let us stop there, let us observe the scene suspended in the gloaming. A glittering film of water touching a stiff fingertip. A steaming human body balancing on this quivering skin of water. A naked, hovering pair of twins, and between them the surface of the water, like a glimmering text, a black and reflective starry sky.

The Earth

6   One wishy-washy evening I was sitting in the astrotruckers' caff on the asteroid Wankistocking. (Something that has always annoyed me in science-fiction films is all those boring, stereotyped names they give to any inhabited heavenly body. They're all called Epsilon, Centauris, or something equally uninspired. Or even worse, a combination of letters that always includes an X, such as XCT, WXQ-Alpha and so on. In fact, of course, planets nearly always have strikingly peculiar names that often sound ridiculous to the ears of alien civilisations.)

Anyway, I was sitting at this plastic table on the asteroid Wankistocking, sipping a glass of volcanic yogurt and gazing down through the viewing panel at the dirty-grey concrete of the hangar where our space-ship was parked, gulping down fuel. There can't be many places more depressing than these godforsaken service stations along the metals-export delivery route. Everybody's just filling in time, neon tubes on the blink, a firmament of brain-numbing desolation, a bank of uninspiring gaming machines where a four-legged miner is intent on ridding himself of his hard-earned wages. At the trestle table next to mine was a gang of miserable-looking yellowyobs guzzling wax – a lot more wax than was good for them. Eventually, for want of anything better to do, they asked me where I came from.

'From the Earth,' I said.

They hadn't a clue what I meant. I eventually realised that it wasn't due to the wax. I translated my origins into all the ten languages I have in my head, and the other 340 lurking in my translating machine, but they just gaped at me through all their numerous orifices.

'The Earth,' I said, gesticulating wildly. 'Where grass and flowers grow.'

The yellowyobs looked even more baffled, and in the end I went to the entrance where the few customers' spacesuits were hanging and scooped up a handful of meagre topsoil from the cactus bed. I carried it back and tipped it onto the table and told them that this is what my planet is called. When it eventually dawned on them that it was true, that I wasn't making it up, that I wasn't even trying to tease them, they burst out laughing so loudly that their dandruff rattled, they wrapped their tentacles round each other and swayed back and forth and snorted so violently that wax sloshed out of every orifice. Finally the miner turned round and enquired as to what was so bloody funny, and they told him that I came from the Earth and they pointed at my little pile of earth, and he started roaring with laughter as well, hooting and chortling and guffawing until his gambling chips sprayed all round the room like a hailstorm.

What to do?

'Wankistocking!' I said, and tried to guffaw back at them, but nobody got the joke, even though it was a much funnier name.

'The Earth,' shrieked the yellowyobs so loudly that the pile of earth was blown away by a hurricane of snorting. And I had no alternative but to leave. I couldn't possibly stay. I went up to the heavily made-up hairball at the cash desk and took out my electronic credit pin, but then I noticed that she too was laughing so much that she nearly fell off her hook, and between her outbursts she tried to gasp that it was on the house, she'd never experienced anything so funny in all her life and no doubt wouldn't do so again until I returned another time, and what was it my planet was called again?

'The Earth, for fuck's sake.'

That made it even worse. They were all rolling in the aisles, a dregsgob at the next table joined in, as did a group of skinspiders hunched over their plates of larvae. Everybody was throwing fits, starting to liquidise and dissolve round the edges.

'The Earth!'

Worse still now, even more violent attacks; two of them died, the skinspiders melted into each other and coagulated, and at the bar a tosspot turned shifting shades of purple and hugged his cranium.

'The Earth! The Earth!'

That was too much for the tosspot, who passed away with a smacking noise and a puff of acrid aroma. The remaining yellowyobs were also on their last legs and I thought: if I say the Earth one more time, I'll kill the lot of them. And so I said:

'The Earth!'

They all sobbed and imploded and flailed around with their limbs in that spastic way of theirs, and I thought bugger this for a lark, I must get away from here, or I'll do away with the lot of them, I mustn't say the Earth any more, and so I said:

'The Earth!'

It was a massacre, and I scarpered and headed for the space truck and started the engine and took off and left the planet Wankistocking, determined never to set foot there again.

They issued a warrant on grounds of mass murder, claiming that I'd slaughtered them all with a laser gun; and when they eventually caught up with me I was in a right pickle. I was put on trial, and the only witness was the hairball from the caff, who'd been maimed for life. When the judge asked me for my version, I said I came from the planet Earth. The judge dissolved into fits of laughter, all the lawyers and jurors as well, and the public, and the security guards and the secretaries, and in the middle of all the chaos the hairball died, shaking with laughter; so I made a dash for it, past the guards who were in a writhing heap, helpless with laughter. I didn't want any more lives on my conscience.

'The Earth!' I yelled, to give myself a bit of a head start, and I managed to thumb a lift with an astrotruck, and ever since I have steered well clear of that corner of the galaxy.

Ponorers

There will always be adventurers. Odd characters who can never settle down. Who are always on the move, who can never take it easy, who always stand with one foot raised. If they see a mountain, they must climb it; if they see a ravine, they must descend into it; if a storm blows up, they must stand facing into the wind. They have a constant itch. Sometimes they achieve the impossible, and the sun suddenly lights up their faces. Then they soon feel empty and bored, fed up and frustrated. They want to be in love, but happiness bores them. Life has to hurt them. Their skin must be chafed by climbing-ropes and harnesses. Their shock of hair has to be windswept. The world is too small for them, growing smaller and smaller; every post they are appointed to and every duty they undertake turns into a straitjacket that restrains and constricts them.

They are the sort of people who, once upon a time,

dared to approach fire; who started hunting animals bigger than themselves; who regarded every desert, every mountain range, every ocean as a challenge. An itch, impossible to ignore.

When space became accessible, it seemed to be waiting for adventurers to come along. At first, of course, the technical problems got in the way. And the costs. A spaceship was as expensive as a skyscraper, and astronauts were highly disciplined, highly trained, highly unusual commando types.

But then the mining operations started. Concessions were sold off for the moon and Mars and several asteroids, and space truckers started commuting. The astrotrucker profession was born. And bit by bit, as technical problems were overcome and increasingly modern spaceships and shuttles came into use, an expanding second-hand market in odds and ends of space hardware sprang up. It suddenly became possible for the man in the street to buy himself a spaceship. Usually a rickety old banger of a spaceship, but if you were a bit of a DIY buff, it was possible to repair most things. Now the space docks were swarming with sinewy youths covered in tattoos, limping old men with Hemingway beards, skinny girls with pistol holsters and needle scars, silent old spinsters with shaven heads and cosmetic mastectomies. All of them were messing about with their own banger. They would lie on their backs welding at awkward angles or stand leaning over skeins of spider's-web electronics with a magnifying glass, cursing and swearing at some heat shield or other that had melted and needed replacing, installing portable greenhouses, dry shower cubicles, gravitation gyros, uploading pornographic videos, solar wind traps, surgical kits for self-operations and the accompanying medical instruction manuals, moisture absorbers for converting sweat and body fluids into drinking water, and all the other essentials for a long voyage.

Then they would set off. Alone. Silent and unobtrusive. Sometimes nobody even realised they had left, they just weren't there any more. Gobbled up by space.

Occasionally you would hear from them. Several months later, a rasping, desperate message would be picked up from an emergency transmitter:

'Help, hel . . . generator bro . . . drifting ab . . . water soon fin . . . help me, help, hel . . .'

Earth would send a radio message to the adventurer in distress somewhere in the solar system with the return coordinates that would enable him to get back home. But he would never be heard from again. His emergency power supply would have run out. Poor bastard.

In the early days the risks really were colossal. We astrotruckers merely shook our heads as we sailed past their dimly lit old wrecks in the darkness of outer space, scarred by cosmic dust and singed by cosmic radiation. We could just about make out some half-awake character in the cockpit, his cowboy-booted feet on the instrument panel, his earphones filled with Bob Dylan and his face made shiny by stale body fat. We had our own nickname for them: we called them piss-drinkers. Their desalination machines were of the cheaper sort, and the water that was constantly being recovered by the moisture absorbers acquired a distinct tang of urine after only a few weeks. As time passed by the whole spaceship was transformed into a stinking, seething can of fermented Baltic herring. The plain fact was that the stench in a shuttle that has been underway for a year or so was so foul that anybody entering it from the outside would immediately be rendered comatose. But the piss-drinkers themselves became as one with the smell. They got used to it.

During the first few years only a few travellers succeeded in returning, in landing their old banger on Mother Earth once more and staggering out, giddy and unsteady. Their foul stench meant that special quarters were soon set up for them next to the main hangar, with showers and disinfectant, where they could scrub off most of the nauseous filth. But most of the adventurers went missing and stayed missing. Presumably they died. Their old tubs leaked, and they themselves were ill-prepared for the boredom and isolation. Most of them were heading for certain death. Quite a lot presumably reckoned on that. As soon as they left the solar system they would shut down the navigation equipment, certain that they would never return. Others had made meticulous calculations for how they would find their way back after ten months of solitary travelling through space, but capsized where no help was available. Forgotten, wiped out. Transformed into aimlessly drifting cosmic rubbish.

As time went by the odds became progressively better. The second-hand spacecraft improved in quality, as did the equipment; and above all, adventurers learned from experience. Several of the solitary travellers who succeeded in returning to Earth published travelogues with titles such as *Hi Cosmos*, *Among Asteroids and Vacuum Soups*, *A Bubble in the Glass of Space*, or the runaway best-seller: *I Called in on God, but Nobody Was at Home*, by Ruben Stanislavsky. The latter is a mixture of ethereal space poetry, repair manual, mid-life crisis and, not least, a depiction of the psychosis that affected Stanislavsky in his isolation. The chapter describing how he spent weeks counting the total number of rivets in his spaceship and then made love to an imitation leather sofa is already a literary classic.

Things break. That was an observation made by all the travellers. But unlike on Earth, you couldn't simply stroll as far as the corner shop to buy a new light bulb. Every loose connection, every little spot of corrosion could be fatal. An airlock that started leaking ever so slightly would empty the spacecraft within six months. A single short circuit could render the whole navigation system unusable. You had to have emergency backup systems. That was the be-all and end-all. Spare parts and tools for making repairs. If the water purification system broke down, you died. It was as simple as that. If your greenhouse wasn't functioning there would be no photosynthesis, and without photosynthesis there was no oxygen. That was a discovery made by many a ghost ship out there.

Ruben Stanislavsky was faced with countless catastrophes, but managed to avert most of them. Once, he was in mortal danger when a meteorite made a crack in the cabin wall, and air started seeping out with a hissing noise. Ruben jumped into his spacesuit and wriggled out into the weightlessness of the glittering stellar system, with an oxygen supply sufficient for a mere seven minutes. Like a ladybird on a piece of straw, he crept along the stays securing the solar panels. Suddenly the spaceship gave a lurch and he lost his grip. He found himself tumbling round and round through space. A helpless beetle, legs kicking. Or as he put it in his own words:

In a flash I was possessed by terror. I was done for. I could see the dark stern of the spaceship looming in front of me. It was speeding inexorably into the night. I was a sailor who had been washed overboard, watching my ship disappear. The last of the solar panels glided past, only a couple of metres away, the final lifebuoy bobbing just out of reach. I stretched out as far as I could, flailing arms and legs in an attempt to swim. But I couldn't reach it. In a few minutes I would be dead. I hoped it would all be over quickly. I decided to make the death struggle less agonising. When the oxygen began to run out, before the pains and cramps rendered me helpless, I would unscrew my collar, drag off my helmet and allow the vacuum to boil my brain. Perhaps my ship would be discovered one day in the distant future. Abandoned, with no trace of any crew. As for me, I would disappear, be swallowed up like tiny grains of dust among the stars.

These thoughts raced through my mind and filled me with despair. I thought about my late parents, buried in the clayey soil back home on the Karelian peninsula. I thought about my taciturn, undernourished son whom I'd neglected, and realised we would never again go jogging round the lake. I thought about newly caught perch fillets, folded in egg and rye flour, fried in a skillet of bubbling butter with freshly cut sprigs of dill, the divine taste of dill.

And I decided to live. My eyes filled with tears. If only I had a rope. A piece of string, the thinnest of cord that I could have thrown at the spacecraft, a loop that could have hooked onto a projection ... I searched desperately through the pockets of my spacesuit. I could feel something hard in one of the thigh pockets. I took it out and examined it in the light from my helmet. It was a bottle of beer. A shiny green, unopened bottle. I'd forgotten about it after a red-haired waitress with soft, pendulous dugs gave it to me in the space terminal before my departure. We had made love that night; she had wrapped her strong thighs round my back, holding me down on Earth. I had struggled, forced myself backwards and felt the orgasm coming on – and at that very moment she had opened her legs and relaxed her grip. The pressure on my back had eased, suddenly I was free. I hovered, weightless, my prick throbbing; I had hovered in space.

Then she had given me that bottle of beer. I had saved it, lifted her mop of heavy, red hair and kissed the back of her hot, damp neck. And I had left less than two hours later.

Now I can see the spaceship gliding away into the night. I hit the neck of the bottle hard against my metal belt, knock off the cap and watch it spin away like a coin. I quickly cover the foaming top with my thumb, then shake the bottle. Point the neck behind me. Then allow a concentrated, fizzing jet of beer to squirt out from under my thumb. It creates a powerful thrust. My body lurches. I shake the bottle again, allow a jet to emerge once more, aiming it behind me. And I slowly start to glide forwards. I gradually gather

pace. I have become a rocket. I have been transformed into a space rocket . . .

And with the aid of this jet of beer, Ruben Stanislavsky
glides back to his spaceship, resurrected from the dead.
He succeeds in repairing the leak, and spends a lot of
time lying on the floor of the airlock, shivering uncontrollably as the state of shock slowly releases its grip.

A few months later, when he is playing patience, the
leisure computer crashes. He tries to restart it, but the
screen remains blank. Ruben never succeeds in
repairing the computer, and has to survive the rest of
his voyage without entertainment.

At first this doesn't worry him unduly. The leisure
computer is just a toy after all, something he's taken
along to help him pass the time. The spaceship's main
computer is working as it should and all the important systems are functioning normally.

But the powerful hard disk of the leisure computer
was his source of entertainment. The superficial stuff.
Recreation. All the computer rubbish he'd scraped
together before setting off. Masses of more or less ridiculous computer games. Chess, of course. Half a collection of short stories he'd hoped to revise and develop
further. Diaries. The old photo albums he'd scanned

in. Erotic pictures. Old letters from schoolmates and girlfriends, drawings his son had made. Then there was the comprehensive collection of music – everything from madrigals and the Beatles to J.P. Nyströms and the Bear Quartet. About four thousand Russian, Polish and Jewish novels. Nearly five thousand karate films, splatter movies, spaghetti westerns, space wars, Danish porno and Monty Python. Not to mention the gigantic reference work *Homo Encyclopaedia* with interactive pictures involving the Kenyan savannas, life at the bottom of Scandinavian mountain tarns, the entire London underground network, the foetus formation of dolphins, the development of the dry battery, the SARS virus, red giants, and an anatomical cross-section of the mosquito.

But it had all vanished. It was as if the whole of his native planet had been wiped out. The Earth no longer existed. All the people he had ever met, all the human thoughts that had ever been conceived or committed to paper; the whole of the beautiful heavenly body he had spent his life on, with its glaciers, world wars, beauty contests and sub-continental spices. All his computer games, from mah-jongg and backgammon to arcade games and Tetris, all the petty diversions and recreational pastimes the human mind could dream up – still, it was possible to live without them. Or was it?

Ruben describes how he gradually loses touch with humanity. First comes loss. Emptiness. Then frustration. Fits of rage. Creeping depression. Loneliness.

'The wearing out of the eyes,' as he puts it. 'Every day the same old pilot's seat, the same old crockery, the same old clothes, the same old face staring at you out of the mirror.'

The day dawns when he feels that his retina has become threadbare. He is aware of something intensely orange in the corner of his eye. Then he hears the voice of an old woman. She makes him feel guilty of inexcusable crimes. She is determined to crush him. Soon he also hears a man's voice booming in the cockpit. The two voices start arguing. They keep at it for hours on end, complaining and accusing each other. The colour turquoise comes into view, like tundra ice. Round patches of sweat start to form on the walls. At first he thinks it's bacteria. Then he sees that in fact it's a series of texts. He ponders them for hours and tries to decipher them. They are describing his life. All the things he has done wrong. All the things that are too late to change. In between fits of angst he experiences periods of total calm and rationality.

'I'm going to pieces,' he thinks. 'Before long the palms of my hands will start bleeding.'

It is the subsequent chapter that provides the title for his book. It has to be the most powerful thing I've ever read about a human being's spiritual struggle, with last-gasp confessions, hell-fire sermons, Russian sexual angst and horrific infernal scenes as bodies are swallowed up by fire – not to mention the last whispers of Christ, the absolutely final words, the ones only Ruben could hear as he stood at the foot of the cross and would have changed the whole of the Christian faith, those final three words, namely . . .

But no, why should I spoil the book for you? Ruben Stanislavsky's opus is fabulous, cruel, self-exclusive; it glitters like a celestial sphere. It is not often that a book can change your life, but there is no doubt that it shook me to the core. Reading it is like taking a bath that purifies one's spirit. Or, as the *New York Times Magazine* puts it: 'A darkness that polishes the soul.'

One day, in the middle of a guilt-laden discussion with a bunch of very stubborn, argumentative plastic spoons, he suddenly notices a black spot on the ceiling. It's moving. The movement is strangely old-fashioned, animal-like, not to say Earth-like. The plastic spoons reluctantly fall silent. Ruben clambers onto the navigation table and discovers that the black spot is a tiny spider. He carefully captures it in a mug. It creeps around inside, trying to find a way of escape. Ruben examines it over and over again, unsure if it is an optical illusion. But it doesn't vanish. The whole situation is improbable. After all, it's years since he left the Earth, but all that time this stowaway must have been hiding somewhere. It must have been lying dormant in some crack or other. A sleeping kinsman.

He calls the spider Fyodor. After his favourite author Dostoyevsky, who many times would also lie dormant while suffering from an epileptic fit. Alas, all those novels that had been on the hard disk of the leisure computer: *Crime and Punishment*, *Notes from the Underground*, *The Brothers Karamazov*. The books were still inside there somewhere, stored in the form of electrochemical structures in the silicon circuits. Every single word, every single chapter was in there, like small, intricate spiders' webs wrapped tightly round their electronic cotton reels. But inaccessible. Frozen.

Fyodor. A tiny moving spot. This black mite succeeds in breaking through Ruben's psychosis once and for all. Fyodor seems not to eat or drink, no matter what food he is offered, but survives for month after month, even so. Ruben starts conducting long conversations with him. Uplifting reflections. About dewy mornings in long grass. Silvery webs dripping with dew drops. They sit there together, feeling homesick. And when Fyodor starts showing signs of weakness, Ruben comforts and consoles him. Talks about friendship, about daring to rely on others. To rest in a brother's arms.

Early one morning Ruben discovers that Fyodor has died. He has lain down next to the side of the mug, tucked his little spidery legs underneath him and given up the ghost. As his friend lies on his deathbed, Ruben promises to return both of them to the Earth. They will get back there, no matter what the cost. Fyodor will go back home.

And so Ruben Stanislavsky became one of the few who managed to return home despite horrific sacrifices. Most adventurers perish in space. The odds are against them from the very start. No matter how well-constructed and sealed a spaceship is, no matter how efficient the recycling processes function, there is always a small leak, a tiny little amount of seepage. As the years go by the solar panels start to crackle, the greenhouse becomes less efficient, food production dwindles and the efficiency of the fuel cells decreases. When Ruben's drifting phantom spaceship was caught and docked by one of the space stations, the air pressure and oxygen content inside were similar to those at the summit of Mount Everest. He was found lying on the floor, as thin as a rake, grey from all the ingrown dirt. His skin was purple from all the burst blood vessels, and the stench was so foul that the paramedics were forced to wear gas masks. But he was still clutching the mug containing the curled-up body of little Fyodor.

Ruben was carried into the space station, strapped to a stretcher. The oxygen content of the air was increased and the air pressure made normal. His lungs filled, he coughed, and the nurses saw how his skin colour became more healthy. And at that very moment, Fyodor woke up. He returned to life, stretched out his long legs and crawled out of the mug. Then he disappeared without trace. Ruben's saviour and friend was never found, nobody knows what became of Fyodor in the end. Perhaps he found his way into one of the other spacecraft parked in the hangar and was eventually launched and conveyed to another solar system. Perhaps he hibernated inside some intergalactic deep-freeze laboratory, only to be thawed out in an entirely different part of the universe sixty thousand years from now. No doubt we shall never know.

● ● ●

As mentioned above, since space is so inhospitable, you have to take with you everything you need in order to survive. Air. Water. Food and heat. If a single link in the chain breaks, you're done for. And so, before departure, all prospective space travellers work out in great detail how long their craft will be able to keep them alive, without topping up their supplies. The most incompetent can only manage for a few months. Most people can keep going for something between four and nine years. Once that basis has been established, you can work out your ponor. Ponor is a word that sends shivers of delight down the spine of every space romantic, and becomes a mantra for every piss-drinker.

Ponor is an acronym of Point Of No Return. The point at which you finally, once and for all, bid farewell to the Earth. If we assume that your old banger of a space-ship, in optimal circumstances, will keep you alive for eight years, you will pass your ponor four years after take-off. That is your final opportunity of getting back home in one piece: four years out and four years back, it's as simple as that. Ponor. The point at which every traveller shudders.

'As you approach your ponor you can feel the hairs standing up on your arms and your heart pounding in your chest; it's like approaching a precipice, seeing the final warning notices flash past, feeling the knife that is cutting through the threads binding you to life. For one brief moment you are balancing on that knife edge, with your back towards Tellus and your face towards the cosmos, and you know that no matter what you choose, a dream is about to die . . .'

The quotation is from someone else who made the journey back home, the female former fighter pilot Jekaterina Münster. She has been there. She has never forgotten it. She chose to return home, and has spent the rest of her life wondering if she did the right thing.

Those who pass their ponor take their leave of humanity. They disappear for good. The courage they display is almost incomprehensible. Perhaps one might call it foolhardiness. Or perhaps it is just that itch, those butterflies in the stomach, the irresistibly alluring death wish.

Once you have passed your ponor there is no going back. It is no longer possible to return to Earth. You have bidden farewell to humanity. There is only one direction in which to proceed, and that is forwards. Heading for nowhere. For the vastness of the universe.

As far as ponorers are concerned, only one thing matters: finding comets. You see, there is ice on comets. And ice can be melted to form water, that luxury item, that liquid that restores us to life. The problem is that comets are so hard to find. In outer space, a long way from the nearest sun, comets don't have tails. You are looking for a black snowball against an empty background that is just as black – but your survival depends on your succeeding. Your supplies are running low, the air pressure in the cabin is falling. The water tanks that form part of the recycling system are more or less empty. Every single drop is rationed. You move as little as possible in order to save energy. You lie down, dozing. Your tongue is swollen, you feel sick. Your saliva feels hard and glutinous. You dip your finger into a glass of water, observe the tiny drop. Bright, glistening. It starts growing, fills out, bulges and falls into the dark cavern of your mouth and trickles down towards the root of your tongue. You can spend hours like that, drop after drop.

Then suddenly, pling! Plingetypling! You stagger unsteadily out of your bunk and gape at the screen. Yes, there is something out there! Probably an asteroid, just a stone. No, hang on a minute, YEEESS! It has a spectrum! By Jove, I'll be damned if it doesn't have a spectrum!

You need to wriggle into your spacesuit in a flash. On with your helmet and steer the spaceship manually towards the lump of rock. Some fine-tuning with the aid of the braking rockets and . . . thud! Then you step outside with a spade and hack away at the ice and start shovelling it into the hold. Ice and snow and frozen slush, you shovel away so manically that your helmet steams up. You make a snowball and fling it out into space as a farewell gesture. It floats away looking grey in the spotlights, a knitted woollen mitten jinking through space. The spaceship takes off with considerable difficulty, heavy and bloated like a bumblebee laden with pollen, and the recycling unit starts working for all it's worth for some time to come. The ice is melted to form water. Drip, drip, divine music coming from the water tank. And the water is broken down into oxygen, *pst pst* from the regulator. And the atmosphere becomes more dense again, the pressure on your chest eases off, and all of a sudden the cabin feels like a dewy fresh summer morning, and you have just gained two, maybe even as many as five extra years of life.

If you can continue like this, hopping from ice floe to ice floe in the black ocean of space, there is no theoretical reason why you can't keep on going as far as you like. As long as the electronics don't go awry. As long as you don't suffer from cancer or have a heart attack.

The bottom line when it comes to the distance you can cover is the length of your own life. The longer you live, the further you travel. And the further you travel, the better your chances of finding what you are searching for.

The really big boost for ponorers came with the invention of coma freezers. They were staggeringly expensive to start with, but even they started to come down in price after a while, and eventually they became affordable on the second-hand market. If you had one of those aboard, you could side-step no end of problems. Shortly after lift-off you could clamber into the freezing chamber and doze off, enveloped in a cloud of nitrogen. You set the alarm clock for anything between a year and a maximum of ten years. And so you no longer need to worry about water or oxygen, food or intolerable loneliness. In addition, the process retards human ageing. At a stroke you can get much, much further out into space and at the same time avoid all the melancholy and, with a bit of luck, reach your eventual destination without being excessively gaga.

And now we are approaching the ultimate dream. The boldest and most magnificent of human aspirations.

The dream of creating a world.

One day, somewhere out there, you will come across a heavenly body. Preferably a planet. Possibly a moon, but if necessary you can make do with an asteroid. But best of all would be a planet, of course. Sufficiently far away from a heat-emitting sun, with an atmosphere and water, and with a bit of luck even oceans.

You carefully land your capsule on a beach in some sheltered bay or other. All around you are stones, wilderness, and spiralling clouds of red dust. There is no sign at all of life. You are the first. You call the place after yourself. Or possibly after your mum. At long last, after all those claustrophobic years, you've got there.

You immediately start thinking along practical lines. Are there any building stones to be found? Carbon dioxide, nitrogen, amino-acids? What is the bedrock? How salty is the sea? That very first afternoon you clamber down onto the beach in your sweaty space-suit, bend down and pour the first teaspoonful of algae into the water. Single-cell algae taken from the spaceship's greenhouse. And bacteria as well, and yeast cells. Tiny grains teeming with life. They fall into the waves breaking on the beach and start to multiply. Soon they'll be drifting the length and breadth of the oceans. You remain standing on the beach, feeling god-like. Trying to come to grips with the incomprehensible. You have brought the gift of life to the planet. You have set in motion the process of creation.

And it is the first day, and evening is approaching. And you know that all is well.

There is always something that survives. A few hardy lichens from the rocks by the Dead Sea, some plankton from the Antarctic ice. After only a few weeks you can discern a slight trace of turbidity in the shallows. The algae have begun to multiply. Some of the hardiest cells have survived. And after only a few months they have spread into neighbouring bays. Glittering green veils sucking in the sunlight and pumping out oxygen. At around the same time the first little shoots start to appear in the well-composted bed by the side of the spaceship. You have planted some seeds and spores and kept them well watered. Grass and lichens. Moss and fungi. Some die, but others flourish and grow, as long as you protect them from the worst of the sandstorms. They burst into bloom and produce seeds. And the seeds spread, some of them take root in the surrounding soil. It takes time, no doubt about that. But as the years pass and the wind spreads the pollen, the world slowly starts to become greener.

And you live the rest of your life there. Eventually you feel your strength beginning to drain away, and one morning you fall over and are unable to get up again. You lie there stiff-limbed, stretched out on your back, lying on a couple of sparse patches of grass. Staring up at the sky arched above you – and suddenly you notice something new. The very first slight trace of blue. You summon up your last reserves of strength and with fumbling fingers ease aside your oxygen mask and breathe the air for the first time. It's unbearably thin and smells of iron and pumice. But you can breathe. There is oxygen here. Oxygen from the algae in all the oceans of the planet, from the grass and bushes, a colossal oxygen factory – and you were the one who started it all off so long ago. Your brief human existence is coming to an end, but you have created a world. You have not lived in vain. In a few million years' time all those algae and bacteria will have developed into single-celled animals. And then it's only a matter of time. Fish. Dinosaurs. Mammals. And then the ultimate, the spark that lights up the world. Intelligent life.

And I was the one who created it, you think. It's all thanks to me.

Thousands of years pass. Your human remains turn white and decompose and eventually disappear altogether. The spaceship crumbles away, corrodes and is washed out to sea by hundreds of thousands of rain showers. Soon every trace of the space traveller has vanished. The only thing remaining is life. Creation. The grazing herds wandering through the forests and the savannas, the silvery shoals in the depths of the oceans, the teeming exclamation marks of insects, all the galloping and swimming and flying flesh that has taken possession of the planet. And with that image imprinted on your consciousness, you can take your leave of life, completely calm and comforted.

Other ponorers have even more grandiose visions. When they have eventually found their dream planet and set the life process in motion, they will construct a powerful radio beacon. They plan to send a signal over vast cosmic distances back to Earth.

'The foundation is laid,' is the message they will transmit. 'I have started things off.'

And so new spaceships will follow. Bringing out the rest of the family. Building materials. Cages with insects and maybe birds and small mammals. So that creation will progress more quickly.

But some female ponorers prefer to manage everything on their own. They keep a store of male sperm deep-frozen in the spaceship. Once they find their planet, the idea is that they will inseminate themselves. Produce a whole series of children from the sperm of various men – white, black, Asian, Aboriginal. All in order to broaden the genetic base. And when their children have grown up, as many of them as they have time and strength to produce, their daughters will continue to inseminate themselves. Generation after generation of children will be born, from all genetic corners of the Earth. The children of the first generation will be half-brothers and sisters, the second generation's offspring will be quarter-brothers and sisters, and so on. One or two will suffer from inbreeding, but enough of them will grow up and remain healthy to keep the race going. The human race. They will create a new human race, a whole new world. And all of it will have sprung from the same original womb. Just like Adam and Eve. But without Adam. Without male original sin.

When we astrotruckers are out on a specially long delivery job, we sometimes come across them. The colonisers. The ones who have settled down out there in the cosmos, and started building and tending the land. In the middle of some barren planet with salt-water seas, you sometimes notice a little green patch that has swollen to form an inviting oasis. On a moon with a thin atmosphere and a volcanic core you find cave dwellings that have been dug into the rust-coloured rock – all you can see is the entrance hole, making the moon look like a giant cheese. We astrotruckers admire these settlers, even though we also think they are out of their minds. We occasionally send them a capsule. A rubbish capsule containing a few old solar cells, some clapped-out but still serviceable drills and other tools, a bundle of electric cables and a stuttering generator, some desalination chemicals, painkillers, some vegetable seeds from our greenhouse and a few other little things that nobody really misses. Plus some Saturday treats, of course: a bag of Swiss chocolate powder, freeze-dried Italian figs, a mouthful of Hebridean whisky in an ion bag, and a hot-off-the-press news bulletin about what is happening just now on good old Earth. Then we drop the capsule, strapped to a smoke grenade. Way down below a white-haired old lady crawls out from her cave and watches the drum tumbling down. The billowing smoke grenade swishes towards her and lands not far away. It's the first time anything like this has happened since she first settled here, forty long years with no human contact whatsoever. She rushes over to the capsule and unfastens the lid while it is still red hot from the fall, and the first thing she hears is a message emitted by the little microchip, the cheering of the crew and the very heartiest of greetings:

'Well done! Keep it up! We hope you enjoy the nougat.'

She raises her skinny scarecrow arms to the heavens one last time as she watches us vanish into the distance. Sooner or later somebody will turn up. It's inevitable. Somebody who will keep things going. Who will further develop her process of creation.

Vanity Case

New astrotruckers often ask: Do you have some kind of list suggesting what we should take with us into space?

The answer is simple. Nothing. Taking personal possessions is strictly forbidden. Every effort is made to keep down the weight. Every extra few grams cost a fortune in fuel when you are measuring your journey in terms of light years, and the company is very strict and confiscates from every rookie their photograph albums, little stones from outside their summer cottage, and bags of their favourite sweets. But what about clothes? I hear you cry. They are supplied on board the spaceship – ugly things, but you get used to them. Hygiene articles are also supplied. But a book, at least? Can't you take a book? Yes, of course, you can take as many books as you like if you're not satisfied with the spaceship's library. But you have to scan them into your personal file in the ship's computer. The only thing you are allowed to take with you is your naked body, after X-raying and intestinal lavage. More than one astrotrucker has tried in vain to sneak aboard unnecessary items such as a necklace or a wedding ring.

But you are allowed to take a vanity case. It is an astrotrucker's most personal possession, the only concrete object you are permitted to take with you. The vanity case comprises six small, transparent, hermetically sealed tubes that can save your life.

As a delivery man you can never be sure where you're going to end up. You think your destination is the Magellan Clouds, you set off, and there are routes and timetables you're supposed to stick to. But all too often the unexpected happens. A technical breakdown, space pirates, a big increase in customs duties or some political development or other forces you to take some never-ending alternative route. A lot of astrotruckers never get to see the Earth again. As a sixteen-year-old you might get a job as a deck hand on a local ferry in order to earn a bit of pocket money during the school holidays, but then your spaceship is impounded at a nearby space station because of some union dispute, and so you try to thumb a lift home and find yourself heading off in entirely the wrong direction. And before you know where you are, you're ten thousand light years away from the Earth. You don't get back home until you're a wrinkled old man, and only then if you're lucky. You find your parents died ages ago, and you are filled with deep melancholy when you hear the birch trees sighing and the thrushes singing for one last time.

That is why the vanity case is compulsory. You must have it with you, no matter how short your voyage is. You might need it sooner than you think. It can inspire you with hope and the will to live, release you from a crippling state of depression or restore within you that giddy feeling of being alive.

In your vanity case you can fill six different tubes with whatever you are going to miss most of all when you leave the Earth behind. Everything is allowed. Almost. (You would have thought people would use a bit of common sense, but there's always some idiot who tries to take explosive paste, enriched uranium or smallpox spores.)

Six little personal mementoes, a few grams of each, and you have the whole of the Earth to choose from, the planet where you were born but might never see again. Six things. It's up to you.

A lot of people choose to take some earth with them.

Ordinary soil. Often from a particular place, such as the wild strawberry patch at their summer cottage, the plant pot with geraniums on Grandma's bedroom window ledge, or the country churchyard in your home village, as often as not with some instructions attached:

'If I die while out in space, my last wish is to be vacuum dried and ground down and mixed with this soil from my home and that my remains be then scattered in the direction of the Earth / on the nearest heavenly body / under a flowering tree on the nearest heavenly body with organic life / where the hell you like, but not in the spaceship's compost bin.'

Strangely enough, it's almost as popular to take with you some shit. You might turn your nose up at that, but we experienced astrotruckers understand what the point is. The smell. There are few things that clear a muddled brain out in space like the smell of good, honest manure. We Scandinavians seem to prefer cowshit. The smell of a steaming cowpat can set our eyes sparkling and fill our hearts with longing. The pastures of our childhood, mosquito-bitten legs, the buzzing of bumble bees, strawberries and milk in a bowl in the newly mown grass. Other cultures prefer camel shit, or maybe the shit of a horse or a donkey, or even a rhesus monkey. Really seasoned astrotruckers take – you may find this hard to believe – human excrement. Usually their own. Before they leave home they have one last, favourite dinner. It might be pickled herring and potatoes to start with, for instance, then meatballs fried in butter, brown beans with pork, diced chicken with curry sauce, spare ribs baked in mustard, a piece of pepperoni pizza and jambalaya drenched in cayenne pepper with prawns and for afters, real vanilla ice cream with cola sauce and coffee and to round it all off a little wafer-thin square of delicate mint chocolate.

The next day you duly do your business, and poke a few pinches of the result into one of the tubes. This might sound shocking if you have never been in the cosmos, but the fact is, as every experienced astrotrucker knows, your faeces smell quite different when you're travelling through space. It has to do with the food you eat out there, of course. After only a few weeks, every motion you produce smells of old plastic: a mixture of burnt brake lining, sewing machine oil and paracetamol. After a while you might start hating your body. Start to feel you are no longer human. In that case the tube could be your saviour: a little sniff, an outside dry closet with a heart on the door, and you feel as if you're standing on solid ground once more.

Soil and dung. Four tubes to go.

Some people take with them something to eat. There's only room for a tablespoonful, but what counts is the memory. Remembering the taste. As I come from Tornedalen, I've tried taking cloudberry jam in order to call up, when I close my eyes, that sun-drenched northern swamp oozing golden steam. Or a few flakes of dried reindeer meat. Sun-dried under the eaves in the early spring in Mukkakangas as the icicles are starting to drip with brilliantly clear drops of the winter's snow. Others prefer fish. It is almost impossible to reproduce the taste of fish in an artificial space kitchen, and especially Norwegians, Portuguese and Japanese like to take with them a piece of tightly rolled fish skin that they can gnaw or suck at when they are feeling really desperate. Some connoisseurs want to have a few drops of Beerenburg schnapps from Friesland, or a sip of the hundred-year-old cognac they are looking forward to supping when they celebrate their fiftieth birthday. Others prefer tobacco. The tube in the vanity case only holds one compressed cigarette, or you can press in a couple of portions of snuff. I have seen nicotine addicts take out their vanity case and stare at that crumpled up ciggy with an expression of such ardent passion that the whole of their body was shaking. Only once would they be able to light it. Only once during their circumnavigation of the universe. With tears in their eyes they will smoke that crumpled cigarette, lying naked on the divan in the panorama cabin with all the lights switched off, and all the stars of the galaxy like millions of needles out there in space as the nicotine sticks its white claws into every single pore of their skin.

Those who have left a family back home sometimes take with them a lock of their fiancée's or husband's hair. But that sometimes only seems to make their homesickness even worse. As does breathing in the baby smell of their newly born daughter, and being forced to realise that the child will have grown up and become a stranger by the time they get back.

Those with a more spiritual disposition want to take some holy water from the Ganges with them. Or from the Nile, or even from the River Torne. Others prefer some tears from a weeping icon. Or holy water blessed by the Pope. Some travellers take some ashes with them, and claim that it's because of the smell – but in ninety per cent of cases they are in fact the ashes of some relative who asked to have a bit of themselves scattered in space. Officially, that is forbidden. But in practice there are several multimillionaires who have had the whole of their ashes scattered in the cosmos by means of bribing a few hundred astrotruckers to take with them a gram or two in their vanity case. I can understand the appeal of that. Having your body scattered all over the oceans and inlets of space like a grey, incredibly thin but extensive wisp of smoke, millions of light years from end to end.

Somebody once wrote a doctoral thesis about vanity cases. It contained a long list of what thousands of astrotruckers had taken with them in their little tubes: scorpion tails, pine resin, aviation fuel, clover nectar, cinnabar, tiger balsam, house flies, arrowheads, narwhal oil, sandalwood, argon, surf, marzipan, chicken blood, graphite, mouse paw, Seville orange, red Falun paint, coffee, amalgam, betel nut, soft soap, eucalyptus, feathers from a bird of paradise . . .

One astrotrucker had a tube that was completely empty. When the researcher asked her about it, she explained that the tube had been standing open on her garden table one evening in August while she watched the sun gradually set behind islands in the archipelago. It had been warm. An arctic tern had been circling over her head, dived down behind a rock and then come back up again. There was a fresh smell of seaweed and algae, and a trace of salt in the air.

She had closed the tube, at that point, at that very moment. She explained that it contained happiness.

Stone

Pernilla Hamrin was a difficult person. Like all difficult persons she maintained that it was the world around her that was difficult. The only thing she ever tried to do was to put matters to rights. Point out obvious faults. Continue to do the right thing despite the fact that everybody else was getting it wrong.

Like so many pedants and know-alls, she had grown up in a religious environment. Her father had been a pastor in the Pentecostal Church, and she still had that typical free-church air, vaguely reproachful, with her eyebrows slightly raised, lips pursed and head raised haughtily, frequently cocked to one side.

'Do you really not see?' her expression seemed to be saying. 'Haven't the scales fallen from your eyes?'

Pernilla was thin as a rake and at the moment she smelled of sulphur, as she had been fasting for three weeks and her body was secreting waste products. She was sitting in the main lecture theatre at Luleå Technical University, correcting the professor of minerology. He was lecturing on the crystallographic properties of iron ore, and had placed on the desk in front of him a shiny grey lump of ore taken from a seam 700 metres below the surface at the Kiirunavaara mine.

Pernilla interrupted him and started pointing out the unethical nature of ore-mining. How we humans down the ages have treated stones cruelly. For thousands of years we have split and polished them, hit enemies on the head with them, carved them to make arrowheads, smelted them down in order to extract metals, chiselled runic characters into them and placed them over the graves of our dead. This was unmitigated apartheid! Stones were in fact the group most discriminated against on Earth.

All the students stared at her. Some grinned. The professor, who was a patient man, let her rant on and wave her arms about and fill the theatre with the smell of sulphur. Then he suggested they should have a break.

That evening Pernilla lay on the sofa in her student room on Porsön, sipping a cup of nettle tea. It had been a strenuous day. She was leafing absent-mindedly through the latest essays written by some of her fellow students, taciturn theorists from the backwoods of northern Sweden who had suffered their way through yet another term in the chilly, far too well ventilated laboratories and written yet another hopeless essay on some conglomerate or other of zero interest to anybody with the possible exception of their mothers. They were boring to read and boring to think about; the texts were so devoid of life and spontaneity that she could feel her eyelids fusing together. She was feeling more and more sleepy. She was in the no-man's-land between alertness and slumber and could feel her thoughts beginning to wander around of their own accord. And she found herself meditating on the question:

'Why are stones so terribly boring? Indeed, why is the science of stones one of the most monotonous subjects to study on this planet?'

'Because they're asleep,' said a voice somewhere deep down inside her.

She paused to consider that thought. There was no denying that it was an amusing image. A big, old lump of granite lying in the moss, snoring. She smiled for a while in that blissful state hovering between wakefulness and sleep. Then she jumped to her feet, newly invigorated, went to her worn-out old Linux and wrote the article that was to breathe new life into modern stone research.

What that difficult, annoying woman smelling strongly of sulphur wrote was not a scientific paper, but rather a sort of geological causerie for the student magazine *Luleum*. In it she claimed confidently that stones were alive. But the point was that they lived so slowly that nobody noticed. Throughout history stones had passed through three stages of development, namely:

1. The egg stage, what was normally referred to as the Big Bang.
2. The larva stage, when the basic elements of stones were fused together inside stars.
3. The cocoon stage, when the planet system developed. On these planets stones adopted a hard, dormant and apparently totally immobile form.

Pernilla Hamrin maintained provocatively that, in fact, stones represented the highest level of development that had yet been attained in the universe. Everything else, all the carbon-based life forms that had happened to emerge in passing, such as kelp, mites and human beings, were merely irrelevant coincidences. Stones were silent cocoons inside which an incredibly long drawn-out process was taking place. A transformation and maturation, far too slow for it to be noticed during the brief lifetime of a human being. Only after an unknown number of millions of years would the next stage be reached. The butterfly stage.

At that point Pernilla fell asleep with her forehead resting on the keyboard, and went on to experience the famous Hamrin Dream in which she saw six snakes squirming out of the same distillation jar. If only she'd been a bit more on the ball, this could have been a dream image that inspired her to make another scientific breakthrough. Instead it was her fellow student Ferdinand Bullneck from Kiruna who interpreted the dream for her, and wrote a pioneering thesis on the hexa-ethanol molecule, and how it could enable the manufacture of spirits with an alcohol content of 187 per cent – but as you will readily understand, that is another story.

Pernilla's article was published in *Luleum* on the 'Would-You-Believe-It?' page. As is normal practice with student magazines, very little of their content was written by the editors: they were generally too lazy and untalented for that. Instead they usually swapped, borrowed, pinched and stole material left, right and centre from whatever other student magazines they could find, without worrying about minor details such as copyright – especially in view of the fact that the person named as publisher with legal responsibility for *Luleum* was a Latin lecturer who had died in 1952. Since all other student magazines operated in the same way, Hamrin's article on stones was promulgated as efficiently as a lorry-load of hijacked industrial alcohol, and before long it was being read in universities all over the world.

The Austrian student Sigrid Wasser had a mop of unruly hair and looked rather like a weeping birch tree. That same spring she was sauntering around the university city of Graz, nibbling at a slice of apfelstrudel and demolishing the periodic system. She concluded that the old method of systematising elements according to their proton content was based on an optical illusion. The properties of elements had nothing to do with nuclear particles, but depended on the space between them. What dictated the properties of matter was the vacant spaces inside the swirling electron shell. The bottom line was that matter consisted of vacuity. A multitude of small, invisible spaces. When we stroked a marble statue, what we felt was not the nuclear particles, but the spaces between them. We held vacuity on our hands, and called this vacuity stone. Why had all research hitherto concentrated on the tiny nuclear particles, and completely ignored vacuity? And even more importantly what did all these spaces consist of?

While on one of her walks, Sigrid sat down on a park bench for a rest, took out a copy of the latest issue of the Graz University student magazine, and thumbed through it. It happened to be the issue that carried Pernilla Hamrin's article, badly translated but more or less comprehensible, even so. And in a flash, Sigrid was presented with the missing piece of her jigsaw puzzle.

Stones are at their cocoon stage. They are alive, but they are asleep.

Sleep.

The spaces inside stones – in all matter, come to that – actually consisted of sleep. That was the substance at the heart of the world we lived in: every little grain of matter comprised an infinite number of sleep bubbles.

But if this were true, who or what was sleeping? And what were we humans doing? We were surely trying to disturb this sleep. Sigrid thought more about it, and came to the same conclusion as Hamrin. In some far distant future, sleep must be followed by a waking-up process. Who or what would wake up? Who or what would crawl out of the stones' cocoons? Would it be butterflies? And if so, what would these butterflies look like?

Sigrid eventually published her paper on the subject, and was honest enough to mention Pernilla Hamrin's name. Whether or not that was doing her a favour was another matter, however, as the article was ruthlessly criticised and ridiculed by the tiny proportion of the research world that took note of its existence. Just as Charles Darwin had been caricatured in the nineteenth century as an ape, Sigrid was depicted in the Graz student magazine as a stone, fast asleep and snoring loudly.

The following year two young Russian chemists succeeded in distilling sleep in a laboratory in St Petersburg. Both the test tube containing sleep and the stone from which it had been distilled were displayed in television pictures all over the world. The Russians had even been bold enough to try to wake the stone up, but their heavy-handed attempts had not been successful. A sample of the sleep was sent to several laboratories in universities scattered around the globe, and a series of experiments was conducted – which wasn't all that easy, as sleep is invisible. Nevertheless, the results proved Sigrid's assumption, namely that sleep had the same physical properties as the stone from which it had been extracted: the same thermal capacity, the same density, the same tolerance of pressure, and so on. What was in the test tubes was in fact stone, albeit invisible stone.

There was no alternative but to dig out Sigrid's paper again. And also to seek out the original issue of *Luleum* that carried Pernilla Hamrin's article. And when researchers in Chicago and Sydney and, eventually, the rest of the world managed to repeat the distillation experiment, there was only one conclusion to draw. Sigrid had been right. The periodic system could be discarded. The earth's crust actually consisted of sleep.

Hamrin's theory of sleeping stones had now been confirmed by science and spread like wildfire in popular science periodicals, New Age magazines and the usual tabloids.

'Stones are sleeping!' was the message transmitted worldwide.

And as they were sleeping, it followed, of course, that they must contain life.

'Stones are alive!' was the next headline, and sowed the seed of the rapidly expanding Stone Movement. It was rooted in vegan activism, and became just as dogmatic. Its adherents opposed all unethical treatment of stones. A stone must not be split, crushed or exposed to pain in any other way. If stones were placed around a campfire, they must be sufficiently far away from the flames to ensure that they don't crack as a result of the heat. If stones were to be used for building purposes – erecting a wall, for instance – it was forbidden to use mortar that could choke the stone: the only method permitted was drystone walling, carefully piling one stone on top of another.

The macadam industry was stricken by widely reported sabotage. The Highways Commission was compelled to stop using stones to build embankments at the side of new roads, and to use an expensive new Bakelite material instead. The mining industry was exposed to the most criticism, and subjected to terrorist attacks. The most horrific of these took place in Johannesburg where more than forty miners were killed when their commuter bus was attacked by suicide bombers. A video tape recorded shortly before the attack featured two young, serious-looking women dressed in green overalls:

'We are doing this for the sake of stones. Every single day they are exposed to injustice and torture. We must put a stop to this brutal exploitation of our bedrock.'

Within the Stone Movement there were virulent

arguments about what attitude should be taken towards metal. Everybody agreed that no metal should be extracted from innocent stones, but what about all the metal that had already been smelted? Should it be regarded as just as sacred as the stone it had come from? Or was the metal dead, had the stone's soul been lost as smelting took place, so that one might just as well continue to use the metal that already existed?

This was the question that caused schism in the Stone Movement. Two factions were formed, the larger one being more willing to compromise and accept existing metal, the smaller one being more fanatical with members who lived in wooden houses held together by wooden dowels, and chopped wood with almost useless tools made from sharpened animal bones or reinforced plastic. Attached to the latter group was a fundamentalist sect that worshipped stone idols and tried to bring them to life with their prayers. Several chemists and physicists belonged to this sect, and when their prayers were combined with more scientific methods they were eventually successful. As a result, when the stones were brought to life a spherical cloud visible for miles around was formed, and the headquarters of the stone worshippers and all the surrounding area was obliterated.

After this disaster more moderate attitudes held sway. They tried to work out when the stones would wake up and emerge from their cocoons, and as is the norm with doomsday movements, they concluded that it would be quite soon. So far, three designated dates have passed, and on each occasion there was widespread hysteria with mass meetings and public confession of sins, with people giving away all their goods and chattels. On such occasions bystanders were able to make a very tidy profit. But, of course, there is always a risk that the date is in fact correct, in which case those cashing in will be caught committing the sin of avarice on the Day of Judgement. Sigrid Wasser is now the technical director of the Stone Movement's research laboratory in Innsbruck, and believes that the stones will not wake up for another two million years at least.

And Pernilla Hamrin? When the Stone Movement really took off, she left Luleå and became one of the movement's leading missionaries. It is rumoured that she had been invited to the headquarters of the stone worshippers on the day stones were brought to life, in which case she is now a part of the air we breathe.

But there is another rumour that insists she didn't actually attend the meeting, but was, in fact, threatened with excommunication on the grounds that she was too much of a bugbear. This version of the truth maintains that Pernilla Hamrin underwent a major crisis, went to live in a fisherman's log cabin up in Torneträsk, and nowadays scrapes a living by selling 187 per cent moonshine to the local population.

60

Big Bang

In the beginning the universe was created with a Big Bang. Or so they say. So, we start the story with a rock-hard little sphere. Bang, and it bursts out in all directions and becomes a pitch-black space with galaxies, stars and planets. And people are content to believe that. Few people ask critical questions about it, which is remarkable. Why did the universe become black, for instance? Why not white? Who was responsible for that cock-up?

And what about that original little sphere? What existed before that? If you ask cosmologists they give you a funny look and mutter that before space-time inflation (blah blah blah), space and time didn't exist, and hence the question is irrelevant.

In other words, they simply don't know. They haven't the slightest idea.

There isn't even a good name for that rock-hard little

sphere. That original starting point, as it were. Singularity, say some researchers. Or Superorigo, or some such twaddle that sounds good in the lecture hall. So we'd better invent a name ourselves. The slag-ball. Or maybe the ovum, possibly the novum. Or the atom-clump. Or the star-bomb. Or the globule, perhaps the clodglobule. Or the steel nut. Or the compressed cluster-buster.

Gosh, it's not so easy.

Perhaps Origo isn't too bad after all. Origo. Superorigo. No, come on, get a grip. Let's get our imagination working overtime. What's the first thing you think of when you see a funny-looking lump of something strange? A haggis. That's it. Hot haggis.

So, in the beginning was the haggis. For some reason or other it decided to big-bang itself and form elements and galaxies. But before that it lay there calmly and peacefully in its lump and was as hot as hell.

But before then it wasn't so hot.

And before that it was lukewarm. Cold even. Icy cold. At first the hot haggis was a cold haggis and was frozen into its glacial heaven in the form of a cold haggis-stone.

That state of affairs continued for a freezing cold eternity. And the remarkable thing is that during that

.

eternity a spool-shaped spaceship suddenly passed by. Its instrument panel started blinking and bleeping, so it began circling round the frozen lump to keep an eye on it. After a lot of hesitation a floppy-looking yellowish landing craft descended, two doddery molluscs stepped warily out onto the lump of haggis and tried without success to hack some samples off the surface. But it was too hard. Rock-hard.

'This isn't your usual matter,' the first one said.

'It might be a singularity,' the second one said.

'I'm inclined to think it's a cold haggis,' the first one said.

'It might even be a cold haggis-stone!' exclaimed the second one.

They let that thought sink in for a while.

'It's waiting,' the first one said.

'It's biding its time, that's for sure,' the second one agreed.

'Don't try to wake it up!' warned a third voice from the mother ship.

He had been through this before, and knew that if the cold haggis-stone were to show any sign of life, it would be curtains for all of them.

'Can you wake it up?' the first one said.

'How can you wake it up?' the second one asked.

'Forget it!' the third one roared. 'Come back to the ship.'

Nobody spoke for some time.

'I think I know what you do,' the first one said out of the blue.

'What?' asked the second one.

'You take off your helmet,' the first one said.

'Nooo!' boomed out from the mother ship.

They pondered for a while.

'I think I'll do it,' the first one said.

Then he unfastened his collar and removed his helmet. A bald, oval-shaped head appeared. He bent forward and downwards and let the conical top of his head touch the smooth surface of the cold haggis-stone. A hole appeared immediately in the ground.

'Noooooo!' bellowed the mother ship.

With a damp plop the head sunk down into the hole and broke off. The spacesuit was left behind with the headless wet body writhing around violently inside it, then it slowly calmed down and eventually lay still. The second mollusc looked horrified, and prodded gingerly at the ground where the head had disappeared. It was hard and shiny, completely smooth. But no longer cold.

'Eh?' he exclaimed.

'It's been fertilised!' screeched the mother ship. 'That's torn it!'

'By the head?'

'Yes, you idiot! You fertilise them with your head! Look, it'll be boiling any minute now. Hell's bells, we've all had it!'

He was absolutely right, the temperature had risen. It seemed to be boiling inside there, a glowing force was thrusting itself up rapidly towards the surface.

'Oops!' the second one exclaimed.

And that word triggered off the Big Bang. That shout of 'Oops' was the beginning and the birth. And the rest is history.

But let's go back in time. Spaceship? I hear you cry. I'm just as surprised as you are. How on earth could there be a spaceship before the birth of the universe? We'd better ask the most intelligent of the three, the guy in the mother ship.

Interview with the unknown spaceship's crewman:

'Hi, do you mind if I ask you a few questions?'

'What about?'

'I'm just curious about what you're doing.'

65

'Hmm.'

'Where are you heading?'

'Well, that's a good question.'

'Don't you know?'

'It's more a matter of it being secret. We're on a reconnaissance mission, searching the environment.'

'What are you looking for?'

'Irregularities, you might say. Stress fields. Gravity. Radiation. Anything that might indicate a cold hag— hmm!'

'Were you going to say a cold haggis?'

'That's confidential information.'

'I promise not to say anything to the crew. But I have to know. What to goodness is a cold haggis anyway?'

'You never know.'

'Really?'

'No, it can vary enormously in appearance. But they exist in the wrinkles.'

'In the wrinkles?'

'In the wrinkles of space. Little egg bubbles, you might say. Our mission is to locate them and report back, and then Headquarters decides if they are going to be fertilised.'

'You mean a Big Bang?'

'Yes, there's usually a hell of a big bang.'

'And Headquarters can decide if there's going to be a Big Bang, is that right?'

'Yes, that's where the man is who makes the decision.'

'And who is he?'

'That's confidential information.'

'God?'

'Nope.'

'It must be God. Of course it must be God! Who else could it be?'

'Nobody.'

'Come on now, explain what you mean.'

'Unfortunately I'm not allowed to tell you any more.'

How odd. What can one say about that? We'd better go to Headquarters and ask some more questions.

Interview at Headquarters, with a taciturn, cellophane-like secretary type:

'Hi, so this is Headquarters, is that right?'

'Correct.'

'And you are employed here?'

'I report directly to the Boss.'

'And who is the Boss?'

'He's the one who makes the decisions. He sends out expeditionary parties in all directions, looking for secret objects, and he decides if they are going to be fertilised.'

'Yes, I know that. But who is the Boss, in fact?'

'Do you mean what's his name?'

'Yes, that will do for starters.'

'Roly.'

'Did you say Roly?'

'Correct.'

'Hmm, Roly. And Roly is all-powerful, is that right?'

'Precisely.'

'Is he evil or good?'

'Good, of course.'

'Pretty powerful, then. So at the moment I'm standing within a stone's throw of God Almighty, creator of heaven and earth!'

'Who are you talking about?'

'God.'

'Roly isn't God.'

'Almighty and good and creator of the universe – it sounds pretty convincing to me, don't you agree?'

'No.'

'I'd like to meet him.'

'Now I must ask you to leave!'

'Oh come on, just a little interview, please?'

'Get out of here!'

'But just a couple of questions . . .'

'Certainly not! Get out, now! Out, I said.'

I slip past him and start running quickly up some stairs. The secretary chases me with a carved walking stick, hacking at the back of my legs and trying to trip me up. He hurts my knee, but I manage to shove the secretary over a baldachin, and then hobble out onto an extremely highly polished, incredibly white marble floor. A tall figure can just be seen behind a slowly swaying silk curtain.

Interview with Roly. Top management.

'Do I have the pleasure of meeting Roly?'

'Who let you in?'

'May I ask you what your main task is?'

'I search for objects to fertilise.'

'You mean a cold haggis.'

'Hmm . . . well, let's call it a cold haggis. When my colleagues have found one, they'll get in touch with me, and I'll go there and fertilise it with my head. That will cause a bang, an enormous bang, an explosion bigger than you can imagine in your wildest dreams.'

'Oh yes I can.'

'Oh no you can't. I'm not just talking about an

explosion, I'm talking about a temperature of millions of degrees and boiling plasma and devastating energy that sprays out shock waves that are condensed into matter only after hundreds of thousands of years. And a part of me will be in every ounce of that matter.'

'So that's the plan, is it?'

'After that I shall permeate the whole of the universe. It's a beautiful thought. To be everywhere.'

'But why you?'

'I have been chosen by my people. I am the worthiest of us all, the one with most wisdom. With me as its creator the universe will be a fervent place. I intend to make the universe white. Space, the night sky, everything will be white.'

'White?'

'Yes, as white as this highly polished marble floor. Feel how soft it is, how perfect it is.'

'And you are the leader of a whole race?'

'Race is perhaps too big a concept. There are only a few hundred of us.'

'But where do you come from? I must know. If you are the one who is going to create the universe, who created you?'

Roly looks at me without speaking. His bald head is very large and pale, and decidedly conical in shape.

'It was our mother,' he says softly.

'Your mother?'

'The mother of all our people. She's very old. She gave birth to all of us. But now she's going to leave us.'

'Where is she?'

'Here.'

'Here?'

'Everywhere.'

He looks at me calmly, slightly amused. Then he gestures towards the silken curtain. A very small figure saunters in from the side, dressed in furs. Little, naked feet patter on the marble floor. His mother barely reaches as high as her son's knee. She stops, he unwinds all the shawls and robes and long, elegant fabrics. Then he crouches down and kisses her tenderly.

When he stands up I see that she is a child. A girl aged two, perhaps two and a half.

'You call your daughter your mother?' I ask.

'She is my mother. Everybody's mother. All our people come from her. She's the one you wanted to see.'

'But . . .'

I break off and look at the little child. As I watch, she seems to shrink, grow smaller. As if she were growing inwards. He sits down next to her, his legs crossed. She strokes his ear with her little hand, takes hold of it.

'But you are the creator!' I say to him.

He smiles mildly. Rises to his feet and lifts up the little girl.

'I'm sorry, but this is as far as you're going to get,' he says. 'I have to go now, one of our spaceships has just discovered a cold haggis . . .'

'A crew of three?' I ask.

'That's right.'

'One in the mother ship, and two who have landed.'

'Yes, two nitwits we sent out purely in order to get rid of them.'

'Nitwits?'

'Complete nincompoops, believe you me, each even worse than the other. And what happens? They stumble upon a cold haggis!'

'Oh dear.'

'Why do you say "Oh dear"? That's the way creation is. Some beings are very intelligent, like me. A lot more are normally gifted, quite a few are low achievers, but a few poor souls are nitwits and nincom-poops.'

'Bad news,' I say quietly.

'What?'

'One of those halfwits has just fertilised a cold haggis-stone.'

'With his empty nincompoopish head?'

'Precisely, with his empty nincompoopish head!'

We look at each other. The very next second there is a flash of light on the horizon. The light soon envelops us, and everything everything everything becomes white white white . . .

I mean black black black . . .

A black universe. Black as the inside of a sack. As black and empty as the head of a nincompoop.

That's how it all started. The fact is, we got the universe we deserved.

Pause

74   We must pause at this point. I'm a bit worried about you, to tell you the truth. Your face is disturbingly pale and your forehead is tinged with violet. You're not the first one to be affected. A lot of people can't cope with facing up to space in this way. They feel dizzy. Their mind starts spinning when faced with the incomprehensibility of space. Human beings are more suited to life on a small scale, people prefer to live in a tiny nest with white curtains. Sometimes they have the urge to look out, and so they make a little peephole. And hence they can look at one thing at a time. A lake. A tree. A yellowish-gold moon rising over the meadow. One step at a time, not too much or the result will be confusion. They don't want things getting into a jumbled mess.

    But then, all of a sudden, the lid is lifted off the mouse's nest and their little peppercorn eyes peer up into God's foaming, typhoon-like visage. They go weak at the knees, squeak helplessly, and try to bury their heads in their pillows.

That is only human.

Come on, my friend, sit yourself down. I'll tilt the chair back for you. I'll switch on the massage machine, there, can you feel those soothing vibrations in the small of your back? And I'll dim the lights. Just relax now, I'll put some music on for you. Something old-fashioned with saxophones? Some jazz, the blues? You're back in the cockpit now. There are walls on all sides. Heat is hissing out of the air conditioning, into your secure little bubble.

Take it easy now, stop thinking about space. Think of your mother instead. Her calm face is leaning over you, the morning sun is shining in through the window. The smell of warm milk. A piece of soap being rubbed and turned under running water. A pet. The coat of a dog, smelling good and reassuring, like a familiar carpet. You are at home again. On Earth. The blue, friendly planet Earth.

The biggest problem when it comes to describing space is that it's not coherent. Space is made up of fragments. Masses of splinters whirling around after an ancient

Big Bang. The human brain doesn't like splinters. When you describe space, people prefer to hear a story. A long story that ends happily. Or even sadly. But a story even so, a length of billowing cloth that hangs together with weft and warp and threads. People want a beginning, an end, and they want three wishes in the middle. Plus a few exciting struggles between good and evil.

But space isn't like that. It stays blurred, no matter how closely you look at it. People refuse to accept that fact; they get irritated, they try to take three steps back in order to see the whole picture. But they can't. Space exists behind them as well, even inside them, and it's impossible ever to get an overall view. Space is all colours at once, all shapes at the same time, spread out over such incomprehensibly large distances that it will never be possible to master it all and make it coherent.

That's why you feel ill.

Space makes you travel-sick.

A picture painted with every colour eventually becomes as brown as shit. You see nothing. It's sad that the cosmos is made up in that way. You hope to get an answer, that's the hopeless thing about being human: you always want the crossword to be solved. But all you get is a hmm.

That's why we astrotruckers become cynical so easily. We'd go mad otherwise. Travelling through space means discovering that there isn't a story. That's the worst thing, the most terrible thing, the most unbearable thing; and so I'll say it again.

There is no story.

Emanuel

78   Emanuel Creutzer was a bitter man. He thought that
life had been unreasonably hard on him, a theme on
which he would hold forth in lengthy monologues in
the pokiest beerhouses in Hamburg, wrapped in his
filthy overcoat imbued with the aroma of cold pizza
takeaways. Despite his enormous talents, he had not
been successful in life and was condemned to live in
a backwater surrounded by dilettantism. Despite his
comparatively young age, he was regarded in the
Department of Applied Physics as a hopeless remnant
of another era; his mother and father in Karlsruhe
had grown tired of his endless rants; his wire-haired
dachshund had been stricken by an incredibly rare
form of throat cancer and now hissed like a cat whenever it tried to bark; his wife had moved to Egypt with
an olive-skinned diving instructor and the pair of
them were writing a book on marine biology in the

Sharm ash-Shaykh region, as well as letters to Emanuel's lawyer designed to undermine and play havoc with his finances. A lot of the regulars who had been listening to his whingeing for years used to protest resentfully. His life was a dream compared with theirs. He had both a job and a home, they had never even had the satisfaction of being married; life had made a mockery of their existence from the instant the midwife had washed them down with cold water in the labour ward to this very moment as they sat in the bar with no money to buy another measly beer.

Emanuel scratched at the eczema in his left ear, and wondered if it was developing into a tumour. Then he bought some beer for his comrades in misery, and also ordered a sandwich for himself. He was served with a delicious slice of rye bread laden with slices of German peppered salami, sun-dried tomatoes in extra virgin olive oil, and capers. He was on the point of taking a bite. But frustratingly his hand twitched and the open sandwich fell onto the floor.

Face down.

'Murphy's Law,' said a fat philosophy student smelling of sweat, who had failed all his exams that autumn apart from the one in metaphysics.

'Whose law?' said Emanuel dejectedly.

'Murphy's,' the student repeated. 'Everything that can possibly go wrong, does.'

Emanuel sat there motionless while the waitress cleared away the remains of the sandwich, and handed him the bill.

'Another one,' he said gloomily.

In the twinkling of an eye he found himself with another open sandwich in his hand, this time a slice of white bread with roast beef, creamy mayonnaise and a sprig of parsley. With an inscrutable expression on his face, he stretched out his arm, closed his eyes and dropped the delicious-looking sandwich on the floor. Once again it landed face down, on the greasy, filthy stone floor. The gobsmacked regulars watched in ever-increasing horror as he paid for the sandwich, then ordered a third one, and a fourth, and a fifth. He allowed all of them to fall to the floor in the same way, and all of them fell face down.

'Hm,' said Emanuel.

'You idiot!' exclaimed the barmaid.

The student of philosophy hurriedly emptied his tankard and staggered off home in a bad mood, oblivious to the fact that he had just been present at the birth of determinist physical science and that he'd just been treated to a beer by the most celebrated and original research scientist of the coming decade.

The following morning Emanuel turned up early at work, an occurrence so rare that his colleagues assumed he had forgotten to adjust his watch to winter time. He sat down at his desk in the Department of Applied Physics and thought for a while. Then he phoned the particle researchers at CERN in Switzerland and asked them to send him photographs of all the acceleration experiments in which something had gone wrong. They suggested that he might like to go to hell without passing Go. He rang again, repeated his request in extremely polite terms, and received the same answer, albeit more crudely expressed this time. After several days of failed attempts at all levels, he adopted a new strategy. He contacted an office-cleaning company in Zürich, claimed to be the boss of a recycling firm and expressed his willingness to purchase the contents of all the rubbish bins used by CERN researchers. This approach proved to be much more fruitful, and he soon found himself smoothing out crumpled cloud chamber photographs taken in connection with hundreds of nuclear fission experiments that had gone wrong. There were photographs of protons that had ended up in the wrong place, electrons that had gone astray, contaminations and leaking lids plus voltages that had been too low or paper that had been loaded skew-whiff, and there was a research worker who had spilled coffee over the registrator.

'Just what I was looking for,' said Emanuel, and he started scrutinising the documents with the aid of a magnifying glass.

By the end of the month he was certain of it. The evidence was unambiguous. He leaned back on his chair. The backrest creaked rather worryingly as he clasped his hands behind the back of his nobbly neck. His mind was swimming as he put his somewhat confused discovery into words:

Life is comprised of tiny, uncontrollable particles.

After a few days of deliberation, he named the particle Rupert, after his wife's divorce lawyer. A Rupert was laden with angry, unpleasant energy that it was always trying to be rid of. It travelled through the universe hunting for anything it could sabotage. This Rupert was a real swine, and could turn up anywhere, at any time. It would always find a suitable target eventually, whereupon it would spit out its disgusting substances that mucked everything up.

The problem was that a Rupert wasn't visible. Not

in the normal sense of the word, that is. What Emanuel discovered among the particle traces were nasty, black areas, tiny little spots – or rather, holes. They seemed to increase in number according to how important the experiment was, how much it had cost, how great the expectations were. In combination the Ruperts could easily push aside a neutron or divert the course of electrons so that, despite months of meticulous preparations, everything went wrong. Emanuel had appended photographic examples to his scientific paper, with arrows pointing to areas where the Ruperts were especially active. He published his results with a feeling of triumph.

The result was the biggest anticlimax ever witnessed in the world of scientific research since Schiaparelli claimed to have discovered canals on Mars. The immediate reaction was astonished silence, with meaningful sideways glances and raised eyebrows, followed by a chorus of hilarious laughter. (It is worth noting that the canals had actually existed but been wiped out 14 million years ago during the Martian wars of extermination. The latest Turkoman expedition to Mars managed to excavate archaeological proof of the ecological catastrophe that lay behind the destruction.)

The only people who didn't laugh their heads off at

Emanuel were the particle researchers at CERN. They sat and scrutinised his scoffed-at article and gulped till their jaws dropped. Word soon got round in every CERN lab, at every level of research, from the overall-clad ozone-smelling kilovolt electricians to the tweezer-wielders up in the nuclear analysis section. It wasn't long before a meeting was called. Top secret telephone calls were made. The board of directors was informed.

Financial backers. Including the well-known Swiss chocolate manufacturer that was behind the latest advertising slogan: Chocolate without nuts is like an atomic nucleus without quarks.

It was soon clear to everybody that they now had an explanation. The answer to why so much was going to pot at CERN, why such a high percentage of experiments were turning out badly, why fuses were blowing at critical moments, why dry joints and faulty relays were constantly turning particle research into a walk along the Via Dolorosa.

It was all due to the Ruperts. Just as Emanuel had done, they started scrutinising their cloud chamber photographs and they also found those dark malicious concentrations. Black little Ruperts. It wasn't possible to capture them, they were not electrically charged, but it was obvious that they contained a malevolent substance that they spewed forth at the worst possible moments. Efforts were made to analyse the sticky secretions produced by the Ruperts. It could just about be made out as a diffuse cloud, microscopic jets of ink, difficult to see, but its effect on the adjacent atomic structures was obvious. Somebody suggested the substance should be called anti-energy. A sort of opposite to energy, just as the opposite of matter is anti-matter. But the word sounded awkward. Difficult to pronounce. Various suggestions were made, but then the Danish guest professor Laudrup came up with the statement:

'The Ruperts emit misfortune.'

Misfortune.

Bingo!

Laudrup's name for the substance caught on immediately. What they had done was simply to develop Murphy's Law and take it a stage further. Everything that can possibly go wrong, does. Because the world is full of Ruperts that spread misfortune.

All that remained now was to publish the article. But everybody remembered what had happened to Emanuel, all the guffaws and all the mockery, and nobody was prepared to risk his research career. Emanuel himself had taken sick leave after being diagnosed as burnt out, and his alcohol consumption in the spit-and-sawdust beer halls of Hamburg had attained health-threatening levels, despite his epoch-making discovery. His fate was beginning to seem more and more like that of the Hungarian medical consultant Semmelweis, who reduced childbirth mortality in his Viennese hospital by insisting that doctors should start washing their hands, but was harried and persecuted and not vindicated until after his death.

Research scientists are just like everybody else. Superficially they keep up appearances, look serious and prim. But in fact, there's nothing they like more than to talk a lot of rubbish and spread tittle-tattle. At conferences there was always an exchange of gossip over a gin and tonic in the bar. After all the usual chatter about who had been made professor but didn't deserve it, who hadn't because of shady intrigues; after all the obligatory attacks on rival departments, and boasts about their own brilliant achievements; after all the usual derogatory stories about hopeless students and even more unpleasant dirty jokes, the level would have sunk so low that the risk could be taken. There would be a spectrum of new drinks on the table, and the delegates would be guzzling them down.

'Colleagues and combatants,' somebody might say. 'What is the worst thing, the absolute pits, that could happen to your department?'

All kinds of horrors would be dredged up, from the caretaker trying to grope you or the coffee machine breaking down, to the discovery that the buxom new doctoral student with the gazelle-like legs was, in fact, a transvestite. The person who had asked the question let them ramble on until they ran out of steam, leaning back in his chair with his Buddha-like eyes half closed, totally at ease. Puffing and panting, they would finally fall silent. One after another they turned to look at him, their expectant lips coated with saliva. And then he said it. No beating about the bush:

'Misfortune. The worst thing that can happen to you is misfortune.'

They stared at him. They thought he was pissed. And that was OK, because that meant there was no risk in going the whole hog. Coolly and calmly proceeding with the unthinkable: endorsing the Rupert Theory. Describing how the Ruperts spread misfortune, and all the devilish sabotage that came about as a result.

'But . . . er . . . oh . . .'

'So, we have come to the conclusion that Emanuel Creutzer was right,' he ended up by saying. 'Ruperts are everywhere. No doubt your university is crawling with Ruperts.'

His audience coughed nervously. Hollow laughter could be heard, some unbuttoned their shirt collars, others started filing their nails.

'And you suggest these Ruperts are spreading . . . er . . . misfortune?'

There was no need to answer. There was nothing wrong with his audience's intelligence. Inside those well-educated heads memories started flowing. Everything that had gone wrong over the years. Overhead projectors that had broken down in the middle of very significant presentations. Dissertations that had been erased from hard disks. Guest lecturers who had been indisposed by gastric flu. The research assistant whose skull had been split open by a box of Greenland rock samples that somebody had placed carelessly on a top shelf.

Things started happening as soon as the next day.

Very discreetly the CERN researchers were able to start promulgating their Rupert studies to all corners of the globe. To save time, Laudrup wrote a short summary that soon expanded into an article and eventually started to look like a full-blown dissertation. He signed the text with the pseudonym Sergeant Pepper and set about emailing it worldwide. It wasn't long before research was going ahead full steam. Excited particle physicists, biologists, mathematicians, medical specialists and philosophers all started searching for signs of Ruperts. The man in the street had suspected from time immemorial that the world was full of little creatures that stirred up trouble all the time, but it was only now that it became more or less scientifically confirmed.

And suddenly the telephone started ringing in Emanuel Creutzer's home. People wanted to know if he was the man behind the pseudonym Sergeant Pepper. At first he denied it out of hand, but before long he broke off his Prozac diet and started dropping hints that it just possibly might be him after all.

And before he knew where he was, he found himself riding the gravy train. Invitations started flowing in from all corners of the world. They were not invitations to give a lecture – that was a risk nobody dared to take – but to attend completely informal get-togethers. A talk over lunch with a few dozen specially invited listeners. Post-conference parties at which he was able to discuss Sergeant Pepper's conclusions with the sharpest brains of the day. Speaking as a guest expert at totally unofficial panel discussions.

Money started rolling in. Sultry female voices started

leaving messages on his answering machine. He bought himself a new Zagallo suit and a black Porsche. He moved out of his broken-down suburban flat into an extremely fashionable five-roomed apartment in central Hamburg. One evening between his many lecture tours he was sitting on his shiny new English leather sofa, sipping a glass of outstanding Médoc and listening to his new mistress from Bayreuth playing Wagner on the brand new grand piano.

Then it struck him.

I'm no longer suffering from misfortune.

He put down his Bohemian crystal wine glass and observed the blonde beauty as she caressed the keys. He admired the back of her neck: she had put up her shock of flaxen hair and secured it with the gold diadem he had bought for her in Milan, and he could see the tiny hairs on her neck glistening. Her shoulders were working hard on a furious fortissimo, and the narrow, black shoulder straps of her evening dress seemed to be drawn in Indian ink on her pale skin.

I have been lucky, he thought. My destiny has changed. Just now I must be the luckiest guy in the whole of north Germany.

He wondered how on earth it had come about. He didn't exactly deserve it, after all. After the first Rupert catastrophe he had plumbed the depths of despair, gone to pieces totally and started drinking heavily. And at some point during that period of degradation the Ruperts had moved out of his life and taken their accursed misfortune with them.

Emanuel was perhaps a bit slow on the uptake, but he was far from stupid. He started to suspect a connection. As long as he had struggled and striven to be a successful professor and head of department, the Ruperts had hung in clusters round his neck and spewed misfortune over everything he did. But when he was lying helpless and unconscious in the gutter, they had become fed up and gone away.

At first he guessed it must be something chemical. All that beer he had tipped down his throat. Perhaps the Rupert simply couldn't stand the ethyl alcohol. But then he dug deep and forced himself to admit that he'd been doing quite well for himself before the catastrophe as well. The Wagner finale was now approaching on the piano, bombastic, and she turned to look at him, flushed and passionate.

The night was filled with echoing arias. Her nimble piano-fingers round the top of his penis, tender staccatos and tremolos until he turned into one big, taut violin string.

The next morning he sat down at his desk of polished driftwood oak to ponder a little more, feeling blissfully threshed out. Who in our society suffers most misfortune? He wrote down some observations he had made during his life as a series of bullet points:

92

- Younger people suffer more misfortune than older ones.
- Nice people suffer more misfortune than bastards.
- Intelligent people suffer more misfortune than the mentally challenged.
- Boys suffer more misfortune than girls – until they are in their thirties, when women suffer much more misfortune than men.
- Muslims suffer more misfortune than Christians, which is remarkable because Jesus had much less good fortune than Mohammed.
- Jews suffer an incredible amount of misfortune.

Emanuel contemplated his list in silence. According to these points the most unfortunate person would be a relatively young, nice and intelligent man of Jewish extraction. That applied perfectly to him. He was convinced that he was on the right lines. But that didn't explain why his luck had changed. Just what had exerted such pressure to scare off all the Ruperts? Perhaps it had something to do with his lifestyle, the breakdown he had suffered?

Emanuel spent the next month or more thinking hard about this. His enthusiasm for his work grew apace: he wrote rough drafts, analysed, looked for patterns.

Then the ravishingly beautiful pianist suddenly announced that she'd grown tired of him, whereupon she returned to Bayreuth and her forgiving husband. She took the jewellery with her. That evening Emanuel slumped down on the sofa and felt a painful jab in his backside that caused him to tip his Bohemian crystal wine glass and spill Médoc all over the English ox-blood sofa. The jab turned out to have come from a fountain pen he had put in his back pocket, and the leaking ink had ruined his elegant, expensive Zagallo suit.

The penny dropped as he stood in his underpants, trying to remove the wine stains from the sofa.

The Ruperts were back.

I knew it, Emanuel thought bitterly and went out to the nearest sleazy boozer and started knocking back the Pilsner. He spent a week pub-crawling, ignored all the lectures he was supposed to give and tours he had been booked for, and avoided all the organisers who were looking for him in vain.

When the week was up the pianist phoned and tearfully begged him to take her back. The Research Council granted him a generous scholarship he couldn't even remember applying for. The dry-cleaner managed to remove the ink stains using a new Korean solvent, and his suit looked like new.

The Ruperts had gone away again.

That was when it dawned on him. Of course! It was all to do with his outlook. The Ruperts were attracted by some special brain activity, a state of mind, an absolutely unique combination of tiny electric signals produced by the brain, a synapse pattern more attractive to Ruperts than sugar to ants.

The synapse pattern was what is known as ambition. Job randiness. Snootiness. The conceited attitude that presumes you are important, that you are talented, that implies: now, you thickies, stand back and pay homage to this man of genius! Whoosh! That brings the Ruperts flocking towards you like little black viruses, they swoop down in droves and cling onto their victim until they've ensured, sooner or later, that everything goes to pot.

Emanuel spent the next six months studying his

hypothesis, and sometimes had a hard time keeping the Ruperts at bay. He knew he was on the track of something big. The answer to all human misfortune. The explanation for why certain people are affected worse than others, why an open sandwich nearly always lands face down when dropped. It wasn't a coincidence, not by any means. It was all due to one's arrogance.

When the Ruperts were especially problematic, Emanuel tried to disperse them by means of a meditation session. I know I'm not the best in the world, he tried to tell himself. My research is only one effort alongside those of many others. I'm not trying to draw attention to myself; I don't think that I'm anything special.

And it did seem to help. He might suffer from a little misfortune occasionally. But only now and then. The meditation session became a ritual, a regular prayer to be recited when he started to feel too cocky. The Ruperts that were assembling for an attack of misfortune suddenly dispersed. He'd saved the day, and balance had been restored.

Some time later he stumbled by chance upon a similar prayer. But much better expressed. A Danish-Norwegian author had composed it as early as 1933:

Aksel Sandemose. It was an attack on the competitive mentality in society, and he called it 'The Law of Jante':

Thou shalt not think that thou art anything special. Thou shalt not think that thou art cleverer than we are. Thou shalt not . . .

The Law of Jante turned out to be anathema to the Ruperts. Emanuel incorporated it into his dissertation. He made no contact with universities in order to submit it for a degree, but simply posted it on his website. He didn't acknowledge authorship himself, but used the pseudonym Sergeant Pepper. He didn't want to give the impression of bragging.

It was like throwing a lighted match into a petrol tank. The dissertation was blasted out into the world with an infernal bang, it shot like a shock wave of ones and zeros through countries and continents, it was copied, duplicated and downloaded onto hundreds of thousands of hard disks. And everybody who read it was convinced.

Hiding behind Sergeant Pepper was a genius.

The Law of Jante was pinned up on the noticeboard of every laboratory, in every academic department, it was distributed to every research student, it was recited in chorus by thousands of technicians before every rocket launch from Cape Canaveral. Rocket launches had been one of the absolute favourite targets of the Ruperts, after all. Hordes of poncy, stuck-up technologists standing there gaping – and an infinite number of tiny screws that could work loose, fuel gaskets that could start leaking, circuits that could short, condensers that could burn out at the most critical moments.

At CERN they started sending the young and pushy researchers on a coffee break when the accelerators were set in motion. Left behind were the older, somewhat lethargic ladies and gentlemen, competent but healthily unassuming, grey in outline but razor-sharp in thought. They did no more than was necessary, the Ruperts immediately lost interest, and hey presto: the experiments suddenly started to succeed beyond anybody's wildest dreams.

Emanuel sold his sports car, bought a modest corduroy suit and achieved a cult status approaching that of a prophet. He patented a Rupert alarm that could stand on a desk with its long, extremely thin silver antenna that measured the ambient level of misfortune and registered it in a chemical brain.

After some years of measuring he also discovered the origins of Ruperts. They came from a distant corner of the universe and were the result of profound, incredibly intense feelings of guilt on the part of a powerful creative force. For the benefit of his visitors, Emanuel Creutzer used to point in the direction of this force, straight up into the starry sky, towards the boiling navel of the universe.

Thereupon he would excuse himself; he had no desire to suggest that he was any more special than anybody else. He would return very subdued to the drawing room. Someone would sit down at the grand piano, smoothe her dress under her rounded bottom, let down her hair so that it rippled over her back, and lower her strong, slender fingers onto the keys.

Ice

'You can see a blue light now . . .'

'No,' I protest from inside the sarcophagus.

'Hang on a minute, I think it's leaking. Don't move, or we'll have to start all over again. There, can you see a blue light now?'

'Well, more a sort of a black spot.'

'It should be blue, stop pissing about.'

'It's black, and it's making a buzzing noise.'

'A buzzing noise?'

'Yes, can't you hear it?'

'Just a moment, let's see . . . Oh, shit! It's a fly. There's a house fly under the lid.'

Bash!

'Did you get it?'

Smack, thwack. Chong!

'Sorry, I'll have to spray.'

'I can probably hit it with the shroud.'

'Don't move at all! Hold your breath now.'

Pssst, psss-sst.

Cough cough cough...

'Hold your breath, nitwit, this is insect poison.'

'Listen, let's not bother.' *Cough.*

'I think I got the little bastard. Don't move!'

Cough cough... 'It's blue now.'

'Did you say it was blue?'

'Yes, it's blue.'

'OK, it was a bit loose. A bit too much play. Just a sec. I'll remove the fly. Oh bollocks! It's fallen into the shroud!'

'Blue... blue...'

'I can't get at it... Can it stay there?'

'Bluh... blah...'

'OK. let's go then! Nitrogen on. Blood thinner, there. Body temperature 37... 31... 24... 17...'

The first time I had myself deep-frozen was on a mineral expedition that was idiotic from start to finish, to say the least. The whole voyage was financed by a newly formed risk capital company and was supposed to go to a newly discovered planet system with no sun at all. Instead the little planets circled round peculiar lumps of dry ice. In other words, the world we were heading for was ice-cold and dark, guaranteed to be totally devoid of any form of life that could cause us any bother.

I ought to have realised that the whole thing was doomed from the very start. The project was driven by desk-bound yuppies who were only interested in maximising profits before share prices started to fall. Needless to say they went bankrupt before we got back and we never had even a whiff of any wages or commission. And things were not made any better by the fact that these icy planets with temperatures close to absolute zero turned out to be populated by insufferable little helium-based life forms that had learnt how to exploit the extremely weak cosmic radiation in order to survive. As soon as anything warm appeared – us astrotruckers, for instance – they came crawling up like tenacious little icicles and soon built up icebergs around us that took hours to hack through.

Anyway, the journey there was supposed to take a year and a half, and we were given the choice of being deep-frozen or sitting around watching films. I chose the former, partly because I was curious, never having tried it before; but also because the company promised to pay an extra bonus to all those who allowed themselves to be deep-frozen since that would save them money on food. (Guess how much of that bonus we saw.)

And so I was laid out in the coma sarcophagus and anaesthetised together with a house fly, and after that I was gone for a while.

But then came the sex dreams.

The first time researchers heard about this phenomenon they refused to believe it. Most of the people who had volunteered to take part in the experiments kept it to themselves as well, it wasn't a topic they wanted to talk about. It wasn't until the coma freezers became available in the shops and the general public had access to them that rumours started to spread. As soon as you were deep-frozen, you started dreaming about sex. It was said to go on for the whole of the time you were out. One long, intensive sex dream.

It ought to have been impossible. People who are frozen stiff can't have dreams. Especially dreams about sex. During countless numbers of experiments the volunteers had been scanned and sounded in every conceivable way, and all the time brain activity had been at the absolute zero level. The neurons and dendrites were deep-frozen and immobile. Not a single ganglion or synapse was active. The whole telephone network was down, silent, plunged into darkness.

One of the inventors of the coma freezer, a professor of organic thermology from Greenland, Jesper Qaqortoq, decided to investigate the rumour himself. He had himself deep-frozen for two weeks in conditions of intense scientific scrutiny.

When he was thawed out he was in a bad mood and strikingly taciturn. The nursing team assured everybody that his EEG curve had been flat and inactive the whole time. He muttered something, went home in a taxi and returned a week or so later with his written report.

In it Jesper Qaqortoq confirmed that he had had sex dreams.

His report was remarkably short on details, but said that the dreams had existed and were scabrous in character. That was just about all it said about them in the press release.

Reactions varied. Many journalists believed it was false propaganda to make it easier to tempt people to sign up for long space voyages. That was certainly the effect it had. As soon as the general public heard about it, the booking offices were swamped by people wanting to take part. Five years spent like a frozen elk steak was no problem if you spent the time having wet dreams. No matter how intense they were.

So, blue. Bluh . . . blah . . . An itch at the back of my head as the nitrogen mix started to work. Me and a dead house-fly wrapped up in the same shroud. Tingling expectation, soon the party will begin. But first the blue shimmer gets weaker and weaker. Creeps down towards black. I'm falling, disappearing. The coffin lid is closed.

Then there's a smell of cheese. A rather too strong, acrid smell of cheese. Some strip lights are switched on. A dirty white light, crumpled sheets, a pair of track-suit trousers pulled down round my ankles. I'm lying there waiting for something, the trembling minute hand of a health centre clock keeps ticking round. Clogs clonking on a linoleum floor, clomp, clomp. And in marches a woman looking like Hermann Goering. It says Council Property on her flannel robe. She takes it off, her body smells of horses, she's covered in pimples, especially between her ancient, milked-out dugs.

'Polish or Serbo-Croatian?' she coughs out, spitting bits of flannel onto the floor.

'What's Serbo-Croatian?'

'It costs more. Oh shit, I've got a bogey in my nose.'

She pokes around in her nostril with her little finger and pulls out a streaky lump of jelly. The skin of her neck is grey with ingrown filth. She scratches away at her crotch, and the lump of jelly gets stuck somewhere down there.

'I think I'll pass,' I mutter.

But I can hardly move my tongue, I'm as incapable of movement as a waxwork dummy.

She shrugs and sits down on top of me, it's like parking a lorry. And so a long drawn-out bout of intercourse gets under way. It goes so slowly that I wonder if anything's happening at all, and the old hag keeps farting all the time. Now a peeping Tom turns up in the doorway, a bald, naked old bloke who is getting an eyeful while pretending to read *The World of Technology* and slowly, slowly jerking himself off with a gauze oven glove. And at that point some guy comes racing up on a scooter. He's a Lapp and starts yoiking about how randy he is after a five-day stint in a remote reindeer-herding cabin. He wriggles out of his filthy scooter overalls and tries to mount the fat old bloke, but his cock is so flaccid that he can't even get through the fart-ring. A stout woman bath-house attendant appears and shouts that the food's ready, so everybody starts shovelling down devilled pig's liver while I try desperately to run away, but my legs are like treacle. And all the time a film director with a hangover is trying to make a porno film of the debacle that he intends selling to unsuspecting mail order purchasers in the north of Finland.

And so it went on. For a year and a half. Boy, was I glad when they woke me up.

As I said, the researchers were completely nonplussed. Not so much about the pornography, but about the fact that people actually had dreams. If the brain activity level was zero, and it unquestionably was, I shouldn't have been experiencing anything at all. It ought to have been pitch black and ice cold in there.

Before long a conference was held in Copenhagen attended by the world's most prominent neurologists and psychiatrists. They had a lot of explanations for the dreams. The professors spoke in turn about Neuronality, Hypnagogical para-activities, Orthocerebral ESP and suchlike.

Eventually a stick-thin Estonian brain surgeon got to her feet, a hunchbacked old matron with her hair in an enormous bun, not unlike a member of the congregation at a West Laestadian prayer meeting preparing to speak in tongues, and in a shaky voice she declared that all these terms were unnecessary. They weren't needed because there was a word for it already in every language known to her. And that word was 'soul'.

A shudder ran through the auditorium. The conference broke up amidst unpleasant and chaotic scenes, without any final report of proceedings being signed. But deep down, everybody knew she was right.

So it was on the basis of the sex dreams that it became possible to prove the existence of a soul. It was the soul that still remained when all logical thought had ceased and the brain had been transformed into a deep-frozen meatball. When that stage was reached, the soul was left stamping its feet to keep warm, unemployed and unattached – indeed, totally superfluous. No moral questions to get involved in, no conflicts of conscience, no mortal dread requiring a constructive response. And the soul couldn't simply take its leave of the body: the person was still alive, albeit in a deep-frozen state.

Throughout the centuries people have been asking the question: does the soul exist? And now, for the first time, on purely scientific grounds, the answer 'yes' can be given. The soul exists, the soul is immortal, but unfortunately the soul is a dirty old man.

Nevertheless, this was enough for millions to embrace salvation. A new revival movement spread rapidly to all parts of the world and people started worshipping the colour blue. Altars were built of shimmering ice, and long drawn-out prayer meetings were held, difficult to stomach, at which the congregation bore witness to their deep-frozen sexual fantasies, which were meticulously recorded in order to be written down and sold as Holy Writ to unsuspecting mail order purchasers, not least in northern Finland.

As for me, I never went in for deep-freezing again.

The Astrotruckers' Manifesto

It's easy to get on one another's nerves when you're out in space. That's the first thing you learn as an astrotrucker. People are hard work. Hence conflicts come about in every crew sooner or later. There might be somebody who's always sucking his teeth. Who says 'right' at the end of every sentence. Who licks his fingers when leafing through the manuals. Who leaves suds behind after washing his socks in the shower. Who speaks with his mouth full, who sprays the bathroom mirror with toothpaste, who constantly makes his back-rest creak, who cracks his knuckles, who sticks bogeys underneath tables or tells you how all films end.

Unfortunately, you yourself are perfect. The only one who behaves decently. And strangely enough, that's exactly what irritates everybody else – especially when you are trying to explain the worst of the shortcomings manifesting themselves all around you. And before long everybody is deadlocked in a ruthless psychological balance of terror.

You can't go on like that. That goes without saying. When space deliveries first started, freight ships would return after missions to collect mining products lasting several years, and when they were being unloaded the dockers would discover that the crew had divided the whole craft. They had built a Berlin Wall down the middle, divided up the stores and then not spoken to one another for several years. Sometimes it was even worse: one half had simply taken the other half prisoner. Locked the enemy in the gym or the chapel and passed food rations in through a hole in the door. In extreme cases the crew members who had been most annoying were killed. There was an unofficial death sentence in those days, known as the dog paddle. A spacewalk without a spacesuit, while the rest of the crew watched with their noses pressed up against the portholes. It would be recorded in the log book as an accident, and the hope was that relatives wouldn't start stirring up trouble. But it was soon found that this didn't solve the problems on board. Once the crew had got into scapegoat mode, it was only a matter of time before the next conflict brewed up. And a new victim was made to do the dog paddle.

And then another. And sooner or later it would be your own turn.

In its day there was a lot of discussion concerning the military research vessel *Enterprise*. When they returned from an expedition lasting eight years, the crew members had been reduced from 115 to 64. The survivors were in disarray and in a sorry psychological state. They rambled on about an epidemic that had broken out, a deadly virus that had attacked one after another of them, and they were forced to shove the dead bodies out into space because of the risk of infection. But the authorities back on Earth started to have their suspicions. When they examined the spaceship more closely, they found blood stains that had been painted over, or looked as if somebody had tried to wash them away. There were strange scratch marks on some iron railings, and in the cracks between the floorboards they found traces of faeces and blood. In the workshop they discovered a severed big toe that had rolled underneath a safety board and been mummified. DNA tests showed that it had belonged to Alicia Spanner, a freelance film director who had travelled with the crew in order to make a documentary of the voyage. Her equipment was found in a cabin, but all the films had vanished. Closer examination of the toe revealed that its nail had been pulled off by some tool or other, presumably a pair of flat-nosed pliers.

Precisely what had happened to the missing persons was never made public. During the interrogations, the surviving crew members either refused to speak or babbled away as if in some kind of psychotic state. The breakthrough came when Alicia Spanner's films were found. She had hidden them in an air-conditioning duct, and had somehow summoned the strength not to reveal the hiding place under torture. The few who were allowed to see the films were deeply shocked afterwards. The attacks that Alicia had documented with her hidden camera before she was unmasked were so bestial that they were immediately labelled Top Secret. After court martials held in private all the surviving members of the crew were found guilty of first degree murder.

The problem when space travel first started was that the bigwigs kept poking their noses in too much. The company top brass and petty popes wanted to dictate how the spaceships should be run. They were happy to ensure that all the industrial conflicts that take place on Earth were replicated in the space crews. It was do this and do that, niggling disciplinary rules, reveille and salutes and petty threats of wage deductions; it was sticks and carrots, clocking in and CCTV, nagging and formal warnings and disciplinary action.

But they forgot one thing. They forgot that we were heading out into space. Where nobody on Earth could get at us. They tried to keep us under control, but we snipped through the elastic bands one after another.

On the quiet, we astrotruckers pulled off a revolution. We simply had to – the usual behaviour patterns on Earth just didn't work out there. We no longer needed to defend our patches of land or territory, or argue about the position of fences. All we needed to do was to learn how to live in a confined space, side by side, in peace.

That was how the astrotrucker culture started to grow. If we behaved like people did on Earth, our life in space would be pure Hell. And so we started experimenting here and there, without making a fuss about it, and trying new ways of getting along together. We astrotruckers started speaking the same language. After lengthy voyages in space we were able to see life on Earth in a new light. All the old narrow-mindedness. The violence. The arse-licking. We suddenly felt we had discovered something new, of our own. An astrotrucker's approach to life, a new way of being a human being. It was a question of pride. In space, we were the ones who actually knew best.

This gave rise to the astrotruckers' manifesto. The cleverest things that have ever been said about living in space. There are various different versions of the manifesto, but they are all based on the same core ideas.

This is the astrotruckers' manifesto:

1. There is no astrotruckers' manifesto.
2. Didn't you hear, dick-head? There is no astrotruckers' manifesto.
3. But how many times do I have to tell you? There is no astrotruckers' manifesto. If you don't believe me you can stay at home and grow wax beans!

(Wax beans are sometimes replaced by other vegetables that are regarded as being especially ridiculous in various parts of the world. Cauliflower is quite common. Or kohlrabi. Or, for some Africans, babiandurra.)

So, the astrotruckers' manifesto does exist in fact, but the message is that there is no such thing as the asrotruckers' manifesto. Pure Zen Buddhism, you might think. But the reason is obvious. If there were a manifesto the authorities back on Earth would be able to react to it and start forbidding, fining, demanding apologies, etc. The astrotruckers' manifesto enables us to wave two fingers at Earth-dwellers. We are free. You can't lay a finger on us.

So, there is no manifesto. But as soon as we leave the ozone layer behind, it comes into operation. It is confusing for a new member of the crew, it's as if a warm breeze had started blowing through the spaceship. The crew's cheeks turn red. People start smiling. You unfasten your safety belt and leave your seat, take off your boots and throw your shoulder flashes away. The first proclamation in the astrotruckers' manifesto, then, is:

– We have no uniforms.

In many of the fleets owned by the biggest mining and freight delivery companies, wearing a uniform is compulsory. While on duty, you always have to wear their diagonally cut navy-blue collared jackets with matching laminate trousers that have permanent creases and side stripes. Then on goes the peaked cap at take-off and landing, at all other times a steel helmet, hunting beret or possibly a yachting cap, and synthetic boots, unisex model. I say bollocks to that. We take off all that crap as soon as we can and get out our favourite

T-shirt with a jungle print, or maybe a hoodie or even a comfortable, shabby dressing gown. And then we proclaim:

– First names only.

That's our next point. No Mr or Monsieur or Sir, no feudal cap-doffing or bowing, no ranks. All our officers and supervisors are transformed into ordinary blokes and mates. If they refuse, all hell breaks loose and they are subjected to hellish bullying: all their subordinates immediately start mimicking chimpanzees and picking lice from their scalp, and once they've been stripped, from their armpits and pubic regions as well. This is repeated over and over again until whoever it is has been turned into a normal person. Then we introduce:

– Equal pay.

We solemnly reject all the shit-stupid salary scales, piecework agreements and efficiency bonuses for officers who meet their target, all of which earthlings are so fond of. We all spend the same amount of time in space. Is your life supposed to be worth more than mine? No, we simply pool all our wages, high and low, and then divide them up equally. The earthlings generally go mad when they hear about that, both the company and the unions think that we're ruining their agreements, but we just erase all their angry emails. Then we declare that:

– Everybody owns the spaceship.

This applies unconditionally for as long as the voyage lasts. Our spacecraft is our home and our survival, the thin eggshell protecting our lives. If it cracks, we're all finished. Therefore everybody has responsibility for all parts of the ship. Everybody owns the cargo hold. Everybody owns the fuel tanks. Everybody has equal right to the navigation plotter, the heating controls or the computer games. All *No Entry* signs are unscrewed and stored away. Only when we're back on Earth can the company have their spaceship back. Until then, it's ours.

– Free love.

That's what we have. Or so they say. Well, this is one of the most common preconceptions people have about us astrotruckers, that it's all about free love during our voyages. As far as I'm concerned, I can only confirm in the strongest possible terms this persistent myth just won't go away.

– No moaning.

This is the final point in the astrotruckers' manifesto. Do what you have to do, what you have the strength to do and what you have the ability to do. But don't whinge. Don't think things will get any better if you whinge. No moaning. No making a fuss about things. And for Christ's sake don't go round sulking.

It's as easy as that to live in peace. The astrotruckers' manifesto could create peace on earth tomorrow.

'Rubbish!' say the earthlings.

'Take off your uniforms,' we astrotruckers tell them. 'Start with that. Just take your uniforms off.'

'Rubbish!' say the earthlings again.

All right, let them just sit there, counting their money.

The Tangle

The universe is big. The universe is endless. The biggest thing in the universe is the universe. But what is next biggest?

The answer is the tangle.

The tangle is everywhere, like soft, airy cotton wool. If the universe is an egg, the tangle is the fluffy down the egg rests inside. A shimmering fibre packing, so light that it hovers.

This tangle was born when technology had developed to a certain point in outer space. Enormously powerful hydrogen computers had to be invented, and then come down in price until every man in the street owned one. Worlds in every corner of the universe had to be connected and enabled to use compatible programming languages. String-hole communication had to be invented and developed so that computers light years apart could talk to each other at lightning speed. Gradually, everybody would link up with everybody else. Thread by thread the fabric grew bigger and bigger, islands joined up with other islands, flecks spread and oozed into one another, wriggling arms stretched out and found fumbling tentacles in the darkness, circulatory systems were coupled together, and before long this bloated giant began to pulsate and live.

In a nutshell, the tangle is the universe's Internet. All the wisdom and lunacy of outer space is collected there, and once search engines were successfully developed for this mammoth, prodigious, vertiginous gigantic web, anybody at all, anywhere at all, could find out absolutely anything.

(As always, the project aroused the most unrealistic expectations. At long last the little individual would have the opportunity of educating himself, developing his interests, refining his attributes. The tangle would lead to increased democracy, reduced xenophobia, and greater understanding between peoples and cultures. So far the tangle has caused just over two million wars, about forty million insurrections and revolutions, and more than five hundred million new racist insults.)

As time went by, universal specialised societies and chat rooms were set up for literally everything under the sun. No matter how peculiar you were, you always had a soulmate somewhere in another solar system. Clubs were formed for robot waiters with an interest in languages, for molluscs with borderline syndrome, for skin-shedding criminal poisonous snakes or two-legged mammals of humanoid character who wanted to have data sex by linking up with a remote masturbator enabling your partner to click around on a digital clitoris.

It became increasingly common to post texts on the tangle. Articles, school essays, propaganda, pamphlets, everything you could think of. Including imaginative literature. Poetry entered a golden age all over the buzzing planet systems. Short stories and novels were digitalised and made accessible in millions of galaxy libraries, each of which carried tens of thousands of titles, including everything from postmodernist punk prose to Andromedagalactic rune magic.

It was thanks to the tangle that the oldest written texts in the universe were tracked down. They turned out to derive from a long since expunged Azepi civilisation and consisted of short messages hacked into tablets of slate in Mongolian burial vaults, twelve million years before Homer, in the first condensed corner of space after the Big Bang. Unfortunately the original texts no longer exist. The whole cluster of planets where they were created was annihilated later on by a supernova, but before that happened a local archaeologist had made a comprehensive transcript of all the inscriptions. Unfortunately the transcriptions no longer exist in their original form either; they were destroyed by the same devastating supernova that really did go off with a bang and a half. Luckily, however, the transcript had been copied onto laminate rolls on a prison spaceship by lifers who were made to work as a punishment. Unfortunately the original laminate rolls don't exist any more either, as they were used as weapons in the bloodiest prison revolt ever seen, but as luck would have it they had first been scanned into the central computer by a trainee prison warder. Alas, the central computer no longer exists as it was unfortunately burnt up during the revolt. But the good news is that a hacker had broken into it and downloaded the whole file in the mistaken belief that it was some rather unusual computer game. The hacker died while being tortured, slowly choking on his own snot: this was a very complicated form of execution to which hackers were usually sentenced in accordance with the fundamentalist and cruel penal code that was normal in those primitive times. The hacker's computer was ground to dust, as was decreed in such cases, but shortly before that happened the hard disk was stolen by a recycling worker who sold it to a newly qualified student of literary history by the name of Tudor. The recycling worker was later arrested for embezzlement and was executed in accordance with the same fundamentalist law by having his urethra tied in a knot until eventually his bladder burst inside his stomach. On the other hand, Tudor opened the Azepi file, discovered the slate transcriptions, rescued them for posterity and eventually became a world-famous professor and much sought-after guest lecturer. There's no justice, one might be tempted to think.

The Azepi script remained undecrypted throughout the millennia. The characters were made up of a mishmash of chisel cuts and looked like piles of randomly thrown small nails. The guess was that they contained biographies of the people in whose tombs they had originally been found, brief notes about what they had achieved, and perhaps also something about the relatives who had raised the stone. In practice, the task was more or less impossible. Nobody now living knew the original language, nor the Azepi way of life, their environment nor their social conditions since the whole of their world had been blown to smithereens.

A few thousand years after Tudor's landmark discovery,

in a quite different part of the galaxy, a slightly damaged spaceshuttle landed at a scrapyard on the recycling planet, Ura. The crew were sauntering around looking for spare parts when the First Mate, Jacqueline Sande, noticed a stall where they were selling big stone slabs covered in strange carvings. She immediately recognised the script as Azepi texts. Jacqueline had been subscribing for several years to the popular science periodical *Useful to Know*, and in one of the most recent issues she had read a detailed article about the mysterious inscriptions that were as yet incomprehensible.

Trembling with excitement, Jacqueline Sande turned the slabs over and discovered to her surprise that there was a quite different text on the reverse side. It was very similar to Old Linguish. She bought just one of the stones – the patched-up shuttle wouldn't be able to carry anything heavier than that. She eventually managed to repair her spaceship and return home to her mother planet. It transpired that Jacqueline had stumbled upon the biggest archaeological sensation in history. Dating tests showed that the stone was the oldest one known in the universe. The text on the reverse side was indeed Old Linguish, a language that experts had been able to decipher to some extent. It was assumed to be a direct translation of the archaic

Azepi text on the opposite side. At last the Rosetta Stone had been found, the necessary missing link. For the first time it had become possible to work out, albeit with difficulty, the oldest extant inscriptions in the history of the universe.

But what did they say?

You are not going to believe this.

An expedition was sent out immediately to the scrap-yard in order to acquire the rest of the stone slabs. It turned out that they had just been sold for use as paving stones in a big new market, and the would-be purchasers were forced to accept that more than half of them had already been destroyed by stone cutters. They succeeded in buying the rest of the slabs after long drawn-out negotiations – the vendor had realised he was sitting on a gold mine, and pitched the price accordingly. Eventually they were able to load the slabs onto the transporters, and were delighted to find that all of them had Old Linguish translations on the reverse side.

But what did they say? Was it something religious?

Nope.

Researchers set about translating the Old Linguish without delay. But wondered whether their first versions could possibly be correct. Went back to square one. Weighed and played with every word. Cross-checked the

Old Linguish and the Azepish over and over again. Reduced each stroke of the chisel into individual syllables.

But in the end, there was no longer any doubt. The experts were unanimous. They had cracked the code, they had shone light on dark places: now, at long last, they could read the very oldest, the most original text in the entire universe.

The stone slabs from the scrapyard proved to be letters. Very short letters. On the first one, it said quite simply:

'We want better programmes.'

The astonished researchers turned to the other slabs.

'More excitement and feature films.'

'Programmes about love and being betrayed.'

'Give us better films, or we shall stop producing bark.'

And so it went on in a similar fashion. The stone letters from the Azepi planet must have been sent away via some visiting spaceship. They must have made contact with a much more highly developed civilisation that in some way or other exchanged entertainment programmes for some kind of valuable bark. The stone slabs had escaped destruction in the supernova explosion by being transported outside the solar system, presumably to some state archive. As time went by the archive must have fallen into disuse and the stone slabs been sent away, to end up eventually in the scrapyard. And here they were now, the last extant remains of the ancient Azepi civilisation.

With the aid of the translations, it was now at last possible to get to grips with Tudor's transcripts from the old grave slabs. This was a bit more awkward. But after prolonged efforts by the most prominent linguistic experts and ingenious linguistic software, the following messages were deciphered. These were the lines discovered in the Mongolian sepulchres that now, after a long sequence of extraordinary coincidences, could be preserved for posterity:

'Empty guts annoy the blind man.'
'Bluebottles eat ancient feet.'
'Heads are full of bark and weeping.'
'Mummy drills into your ear.'

And on the very last of the slabs it said simply:

'Whoever reads this is an idiot.'

Er, yes. A headache for the academics. After the initial awkward silence, various tentative interpretations were put forward. A bald-headed professor emeritus assumed it was about perverse behaviour. The sepulchres were no doubt in fact macabre brothels. A wizened female etymologist protested and suggested it was about grotesque execution practices, reminiscent of what had happened to the unfortunate hacker. One of the younger female linguists then stood up, tapped her index fingernail on the table and commiserated with all the old fogeys who couldn't see the wood for the trees: this was poetry, of course. A naive, primitive lyric form with links to proverbs and old sayings, in the same tradition as the *Kalevala* or the Icelandic *Edda*.

The enthusiasm and youthful energy of this linguist eventually attracted a large number of disciples, and soon a few authors started writing primitive Azepi poetry. It was a romantic search for the narrative roots of our universe soon after the Big Bang, when the language was fresh and wet and could still be kneaded.

But nobody ever hit upon the correct interpretation. I said you weren't going to believe this. The universe's oldest preserved text, the inscriptions in the Mongolian sepulchres, that is. Was. Wait for it. Here it comes, now the secret will be revealed.

They were the titles of the most popular television

series of the time. The vaults were not sepulchres after all, but were in fact the Azepi civilisation's highly respected television archives. Under every stone slab lay binarily compressed recordings of the two hundred or so episodes each series generally comprised. *Whoever Reads This Is an Idiot* was, incidentally, the most popular series, and was about a bark-chewing firm, and abounded in intrigues and bed-hopping and a lot of comedy concerning the bachelor Pau, who was dogged by bad luck as he tried to find himself a wife, and also starring his dominant mum. There was an outcry when the series was axed, the Azepi revolted and threatened to stop selling bark to aliens and put forward their demands in stone letters that eventually ended up in the scrapyard. When a negotiating delegation landed with fifty newly recorded episodes featuring Pau, the mood was so inflamed that the spaceship was mobbed and all its crew and passengers were killed. The discs were destroyed in the tumult, the aliens never returned and the Azepi population never saw the last episode in which Pau finally married the outstanding beauty of the bark-producing camp, Lou, while the workers stood in a circle clapping and cheering and holding at bay Pau's furious, fuming mum.

● ● ●

Many people predicted that the tangle would be the death of literature. With so many pages to click on, people would no longer have any time to read real books. Soon, surfing would take over and the reading of books would cease, just as gladiatorial contests and the burning of witches had come to an end.

In fact, however, precisely the opposite happened. The site publib.com became one of the most popular and reading exploded in all parts of the universe. The reason for the massive interest was, of course, the enormous range of choice. All of a sudden, absolutely everything had become accessible. All conceivable tastes in every part of the universe could be satisfied. Translation software was being refined all the time, and you could even influence the style yourself. Neutral humdrum prose could be made more hard-boiled or more naivist, flowery and old-fashioned or contemporary and pruned back. Impatient readers could use a summariser that cut out monotonous nature descriptions, dull monologue and other things that didn't carry the story forward. At the other end of the scale was a regurgitation function that made it possible for a favourite novel never to end, but to go on and on for ever with voluptuous little variations. Filters also became popular. Some things that were enjoyed on one planet were taboo on another and if you didn't approve of blasphemy or sodomy between invertebrates, you could engage a whoa-there-filter that cleaned up the text and rendered it harmless. Instead of 'Goddamn', the translation would use 'God be praised' or 'By Jove', or if the religious filter was turned up to maximum, 'I say, what dashed bad luck!'

And so, thanks to the tangle, the reading of books reached its highest level in the history of the world.

But on the other hand, authors vanished.

I say, what dashed bad luck, you might think. And also that it was rather odd – how on earth could that add up?

The Norwegian Guttorm Loll was the first earthling to make the revolutionary discovery. He taught Norwegian at a high school in Tromsö. In his spare time he was an enthusiastic amateur poet with several creative writing courses under his belt, and one of his dreams was to publish a collection of poems of his own. The moment term started, he had Andrea, the new, exotically beautiful school psychologist, in his sights. She had high Indian cheekbones, and her eyes were big and black as if remembering some past terror. She was on her guard. Like an animal that didn't want to be caught. Somewhat awkwardly he sat down opposite her in the staffroom, intending to start a conversation. His stomach was churning as he opened his lunch box: sandwiches with brown cheese and mackerel in tomato sauce. She was silent, crunching away at her olive salad, looking slightly worried as she wrapped her lips round the oily kalamata olives, forming them into a little 'o' as she spat out the spool-shaped stones. He had already established that she was born in Chile, somewhere in the Andes. That was why she had settled in Norway. The mountain peaks, the clear white skies. He wanted to touch her, but was restrained by her evasive manner. She had left a wicked husband, she mentioned one day when he brought her a cup of coffee. A very wicked husband. And then she hurried off, just as he was going to place his little finger against hers.

There was only one thing to do. He must write a poem for her, edge his way into her heart. Your long, black hair is like showers of rain in the night . . . no, like a cascade of sorrow . . . no, more like fur, the fur of something dark and supple, the dark velvet of a panther in the shadowy jungle . . . a tender, soulful poem that would move her, thaw her out and make her realise that behind his patterned cardigan and all-too-early bald head, those crooked front teeth and tass)elled loafers, was a burning – nay, boiling volcano.

The opening was always hardest. The first line. It must grab her attention immediately, prevent her from turning away, persuade her shyly to remove her handbag from the chair beside her to make room for him, get her chin to rise, revealing the cocoa-coloured skin of her neck against the white of her blouse and the gold crucifix glimmering down there, the metal warm against her body, glimmering like a drop of golden saliva . . .

Guttorm crossed his legs to press down the throbbing lump inside his trousers. He closed his eyes and tried to summon pent-up anger, tried to become more southern. Andrea must be convinced that he was piquant spice, not Nordic ice.

He picked up his pen. Now.

'I taste the sweetness of your ripened fruit . . .'

No. For Christ's sake.

'Your valleys bloom lush as I dance on your hills . . .'

Well, there's a touch of Latin passion there all right. But a bit too obvious, perhaps.

> I am the wick in your perfumed oil
> sparks fly from my heart, burst into flame

> my body is licked by raging fire
> I wait in trembling pain

Hmm. Passionate, but too back-heavy. It doesn't take off, it's too whining. But the first line is good, there's passion there.

Guttorm stared at his verse for ages. He felt frustrated, wanted to grasp hold of the words like you do with a rubber film, stretch them out so that they grew in all directions until they covered the whole of the Tromsö sky: I am the wick in your perfumed oil!

Feeling restless, he opened his surfing software and felt that brief moment of giddiness he always experienced when the tangle's logo came up on the screen: a spiral galaxy rotating alongside thousands of other spiral galaxies to form a stylised T. He logged into the search engine, an especially powerful one the school subscribed to, and saw the cursor blinking in a little box.

'I am the wick in your perfumed oil,' he typed. Return.

Blink, blink. Wait . . .

Bingo! A long list of hits. He clicked on the first one. And soon his screen was filled with text:

134

> I am the wick in your perfumed oil
> my body is burning with desire
> to palpate your egg tentacles

Guttorm read quickly through the poem that culminated with a really disgusting climax of amphibian intercourse. Even in that distant civilisation some amateur scribe had formulated the same first line as Guttorm. He clicked on the next hit:

> I am the wick in your perfumed oil
> I am the psi factor in your antigravitational
>   compressor
> I am eightfold in your encrypted curved space . . .

He had landed in an anthology of antique texts from an advanced civilisation that had died out a long time ago. It seemed like a collection of formulae more than anything else.

Guttorm sat for most of the evening reading hundreds of poems that all began with exactly the same first line. The list of hits went on and on. It seemed endless. In the end he sat up straight, feeling rather sick. How was it possible for so many people in the universe to hit upon exactly the same sentence?

As a sort of test, he typed a new verse into the search engine:

> I am a biological athlete
> with a heaven between my legs
> this is awful poetry
> but bollocks to that

Blushing slightly he sent the verse out into the cyberspace of the tangle. It took a bit longer this time. But eventually the list of hits came up on his screen. He opened the first ten and found that this text, word for word, also existed already in every possible corner of outer space. This time he felt on the verge of choking. This couldn't be true.

He spent the whole night repeating the experiment over and over again. And as dawn broke Guttorm stood up from his computer chair, exhausted and shocked. It was inconceivable. No matter how peculiar and strange the poems he wrote, they already existed out there in the tangle. Guttorm Loll was convinced now. His dreams of becoming a poet were shattered. He didn't have a chance.

Everything in the universe was already written.

● ● ●

Everything? Yes, everything. You have to let that sink in for a while. It doesn't seem to be possible. You can't write absolutely everything. Language is too big, all the possible combinations a language contains can never be used up, language is the biggest thing in existence.

Er . . . Excuse me.

What was it that I pointed out almost in passing at the beginning of this chapter? What is the biggest thing of all? The universe, I said, didn't I? And the next biggest thing is the tangle. And in third place comes the Godhead, and in fourth place dark matter, and in fifth place comes the Godhead, and in sixth place as well, and then come all kinds of other things such as cosmic radiation, the Black Hole at the centre of the universe, hydrogen and helium and lots of other elements, and after that comes the devil, and after him his grandmother.

On the latest list language ended up in ninety-eighth place. Just think about that. Ninety-eighth, just before strontium.

So, everything, absolutely everything in the universe was already written. Guttorm Loll gave up poetry, and looked on helplessly as Andrea was beguiled by the brash, loud-voiced PE teacher with his tae kwon do tattoos.

Disillusioned, Guttorm wrote a letter to his professional journal *Läraravisen*, and grimly pointed out that exactly the same letter had, no doubt, already been written in several places dotted about the cosmos. (He was absolutely right.) Readers were shocked. Before long, linguists all over the world were sitting at their computers, repeating Guttorm's experiment, and recording the same results. Language was exhausted.

This was a deathblow for all writers. Most of them stopped writing immediately, as soon as the circumstances were proved. There didn't seem to be any point any more. A few persisted for a while, but then discovered that they couldn't claim copyright. Every single book already existed out there, somewhere in the infinite black ocean where galaxies sparkled like spots of plankton. It was shattering to have been working away at the forthcoming masterpiece for several decades, only to click on the tangle and find that the novel had already been published four million years ago in a neighbouring galaxy. The whole of Homer's works existed already, one of the places that had published them being the seafarers' planet in the Nitin galaxy: everything was there, from the Trojan horse to Cyclops and sirens. The only difference was that the hero was called Odynisiviassavus. But in their language it was pronounced Odysseus.

There was a crisis, of course. Unemployment among cultural workers was sky-high. Suddenly there were masses of eccentrics hanging around with no outlet for their considerable energy. There were a lot of messy divorces. Children were abused. Many were treated for depression and substance abuse, or insomnia.

Then somebody managed to prove that there was poetry that had not yet been written. However, it no longer consisted of words with meaning, since all such combinations had been used up long ago. But certain extreme combinations of letters had not yet been exploited, notably Qgff. Some authors started to write Qgff poetry:

Qgffaih
Qgffppluug
Qgff35
Qgffalliu

And so on. But it never really caught on among readers, and after a few collections of such poetry had appeared from vanity publishers, the project was abandoned.

But the enormous appetite for reading on Earth was

still there. So were masses of unemployed authors. So instead of writing themselves, the authors started surfing. They sought out extracts that appealed to them, fragments of text from near and far, verses, pages, half-chapters that they started cutting and pasting on their screens. They eventually produced a conglomeration of strange text puzzles that they published as a novel under their own name. Everybody knew that the whole thing had been filched, but they called it postmodernism and hey presto! Suddenly it was OK. Many authors became amazingly skilful at finding material on the net, and acquired an impressive literary overview. They knew where all the goodies were. Which epic epochs in which groups of galaxies were worth a visit. Which servers had the best book catalogues. Which of the translation engines were most up to date.

Postmodernism didn't last long. It died out like all navel-gazing generally does. All that remained were the ex-authors with a vast knowledge of literature. Now they thought they really were finished. They thought: I might as well get a job at the check-out desk at the Co-op.

But soon they noticed that they were sought after. They were needed. They were snapped up, given pay rises, free spectacles, fitted sandals and sky-high status.

The authors were transformed, out of their ugly brown cocoons crept gilded dragonflies. They suddenly found themselves fluttering around in the top layer of society, honoured, admired, loved to bits by all and sundry.

They became librarians.

The Swill Hole

142   The Swill Hole tavern on the asteroid Nugget is the
worst drinking dive an astrotrucker can drop into. A
gigantic plastic pod, full to the brim with disgusting
life forms, scroungers, loose morals and dodgy money.
In other words, an absolute must for every greenhorn
on his maiden space voyage.

You can see Nugget from a long way off, looking like
a Christmas tree in the sky. It's all the hundreds of ore
juggernauts, clapped-out container carriers, commer-
cial transporters, long-haul space buses and all the
smaller getaway luggers, stolen car shifters, mafia
yachts, customs hulks, teenage tearaway tubs, satellite
yuppies and the occasional intragalactic research expedition circling round in layer upon layer like a big,
twinkling electron shell. Shiny little shuttles swish up
to the bigger craft and then back down to the rough,
rocky core of Nugget, their fire-engine-red, bat-like solar

panels all agleam. On the navigation screen you can see the radar reflectors forming the name 'The Swill Hole' in old neo-baroque style. Tasteless. And the crew sets off without delay. The newly thawed-out members sit there with a stupid grin on their faces, the captain reads out the health and safety warnings, the mates hoover off the worst of the cabin stench and the engine-room babes wriggle into their little black dresses. The greenhorns hover around in the middle of all the activity, lacing up their trainers and feeling their clean space underpants chafing at their crotches.

We order a shuttle, but there's an awful long wait before it turns up – they're under pressure down there, it's party time. We crowd into a silver-plated composite cucumber, somebody sticks a credit pin into the slot, and whoosh, we're off with our stomachs churning.

Before we know what's happening, we're parked at the oil rig down below. The air lock hisses and we crawl out. It's a carbon dioxide-based median atmosphere, which means that the oxygen content is a bit on the low side for us earthlings. We stagger around as if we're three thousand metres up, panting and somewhat out of breath. On the other hand, some life forms have too much oxygen: two armoured beetles start fighting with their razor-sharp wing sheaths before falling over on their backs, pissed out of their skulls. Even as we stand here in the queue, we can see what the universe has to offer. The manifold nature of life. Some greenhorns come over all dizzy at the sight of so many strange creatures, and throw up even before we get inside. They fall over backwards and have to take the ambulance shuttle back to the mother ship with a damp handkerchief over their eyes. I understand. It's worse than anybody could ever imagine.

Down on Earth, most people believe that aliens look like little green men. Alternatively, like lizards. Space creatures tend to be depicted as similar to us humans, to make it easier for them to carry out their treacherous attacks on earth-dwellers in television series. (Presumably also to save film producers having to spend a fortune on rubber masks that are fiendishly difficult to make.)

In fact, it's more like Picasso. Long banana-like spleens with a yellowish powdery skin. Big bubbling tussocks looking like black pudding with lingon berries and a handful of spanners beaten in. Swollen blisters so covered in warts and pustules that they split every time they bend down. Then there are all the sea creatures, the ones who come in through a different entrance and plop down into the aquarium. You can see them through the glass floor of the lower bar: shimmering blue algae jellyfish; floating pericardia constantly squeezing themselves inside out and back; electric tonsils; all the shoals of intelligent pinpricks darting this way and that like scudding clouds and the mysterious spiderweb jellyfish gleaming like a neon light – they have never managed to acquire any intelligence to speak of, but have been bought by their owners as lavish adornments.

It's a relief to see a biped in fact. Especially if it has a head and seems capable of communicating. That makes it easier to accept that it is spitting out acetic acid or in the process of casting its skin. You synchronise your translating machines, introduce yourself and offer to buy it a drink.

But first you have to get past the doorkeeper. That's not easy, you don't pick a fight with the bouncers at The Swill Hole. They are genetically manipulated from gigantic pigs. Sluggish two-hundred-kilo bog swine that originally rooted around in fermenting mud and developed body armour to protect themselves from the freshwater crocodiles that were always attacking them. Scientists managed to clone the bog swine's body armour and make them more or less house-trained, attach fingers and thumbs to their extremities and teach them the fundamentals of police procedures and regulations. But it was difficult to develop their brains: they swelled up to be sure, but generally speaking the wrong way round.

At last it's my turn.

'You got ID?' grunts the monster when I'm at the front of the queue.

I hold out my visa chip. He sticks it into the reader upside down. There's an error bleep, he bellows in frustration and presses the chip so hard that it crumbles to bits.

'Bad ID!' he decides.

'Hey, hang on a minute . . .'

'You herguing?'

'Eh?'

'You herguing with boss?'

'No, not at all, it's just that . . . my ID . . .'

'Get the fuck outta here!'

'Hang on a minute, I've got my passport as well. My astrotrucker's passport.'

'Oooohh?'

'That counts as ID. Just slot it into the reader. Turn it round first. No, turn it round. Be careful, turn it the other way round . . .'

Crrruunnnch . . .

'Bad ID!'

'Hang on, you ruined it.'

'You herguing?'

'Yes, I really do have to argue a bit – you've destroyed two IDs!'

'You herguing!'

'OK, let's forget it. I just want to get in.'

'You got ID?'

'I'm a decent bloke in fact, I hate crocodiles!'   147

'Hate crocodiles?'

'Yes, I hate stupid bloody bog crocodiles.'

'Oooh hoooh . . . ?'

A sort of grin opens up in the armour.

'Yes,' I say, 'stupid evil shitty crocodiles!'

'Oooh! Hooh hooh! Hooh hooh!'

'Can I come in?'

'Suck prick.'

'I only want to come in.'

'Suck prick.'

I ask you, what the hell is a guy supposed to do? I crawl in between its legs where that mauve piggy prick starts to swell like a whole salami. So I pull it out to its full length, bend it backwards and stick it deep into the pig's own arse-hole. It's a trick that's worked before, and keeps the monster occupied for a while, bellowing and roaring away, while I edge past and disappear into the crowded bar.

We're in. The Swill Hole. What a dump. Think Hieronymus Bosch or splatter films. There's no point in brushing your teeth before you come here. You duck down to avoid a gob of phlegm that comes swishing through the bar, as big as a pancreas, you force your way past foetal membranes and lengths of gut, get pollen all over your coat, dodge out of the way of a sticky tongue that's licking up molluscs from a newly harvested stomach. You're sprayed with sweat and nectar and soot and gall and mineral water. There are no free tables. You stagger around in the melee like a loose testicle, sliding around in the scrotum without finding anything to hang onto. Then you stumble, you can't help it, you slide along the floor on your belly, and before you know where you are the sludge toads are on you, licking away. You fend them off with your feet, but they soon crawl back and peck at you with their filthy, guzzling flat mouths, impossible to kick over onto their backs because of the suction fins on their feet.

The stench is repulsive. Just consider the bad breath; some of the clientele are unapproachable. The half-recumbent swamp-sacks, for instance, that belch methane gas and sulphur compounds and smell like a pile of newly cracked rotten eggs. Or the reek of fresh, iron-cold blood from the humanosaurus in the predators' canteen. And all the fumes of formic acid and boiled cabbage and chlorine and rancid suet and whey and lime and goat's hair and old fag ends that hit you from all directions.

You cautiously force your way through to the bar between all the raffia skin and rump feathers, dorsal discs, amphibian scales and astrotrucker uniforms in every synthetic material the universe has to offer. At the same time you tuck your shirt further down into your trousers and tighten your belt as far as it will go. That's because there are clusters of leeches hanging in the murk under the bar, waiting patiently for the tiniest patch of bare skin. They're always keen to get boozed up, but they're also annoyingly mean. So they're constantly trying to cadge off other drinkers. They cling on with anaesthetising saliva in their sucking mouths and quickly link their bloodstream up with that of the host animal, and then they can dangle from your groin like a plum and spend all evening happily drinking for nothing as your alcohol intake increases.

When you finally get there, you've plenty to choose from.

Oh yes, ho ho ho yes!

Special demands are made of an intergalactic bar, that must be pointed out. It's no use just offering strong beer. Ethyl alcohol is massively popular with some carbon-based creatures such as us earthlings, while others prefer natrium hydroxide or 2,4,5-diammonium-alkaloidsulphate or ordinary flat battery acid. Brains are different, after all. A dry Martini that makes me cheerful and sociable can knock a flying mammoth out, or pass straight through a tiny little pinmouse like water. That green punch the stick cricket is knocking back with such gusto in the booth over there is ninety per cent curare. So you have to be very careful not to pick up the wrong glass. Every now and again somebody goes off with a bang, after dipping his snout in a tankard of dioxin or white spirits or living yogurt. The latter especially has proved to be pure arsenic for all the robots with biochemical memory circuits. After the tiniest drop of yogurt they start singing nationalistic robot anthems, then slump down over the table sobbing pathetically over the lack of a fatherland and patriotic traditions, and in the later stages they start fighting one another until their armour-plating loosens and their biobrains, dissolved by the yogurt, splash down onto the floor like lumps of soft ice-cream.

The bartender is a dirty-looking, Dalek-like robot that slides phlegmatically back and forth, swaying slightly.

'Woya want?' it mutters through the Bakelite, and glowers at you from behind its unwashed lens.

You moronic bastard, you think in annoyance. But what you actually say is:

'A dry Martini with some lime zest and barracuda gin and a chemical olive, not a genuine one, and a cocktail stick of Erkheikki aspen smoked over a juniper fire, and the rim of the glass frosted with iodine-free moon salt, and I want it shaken, not stirred, remember, shaken and not . . .'

Ping! It's on the counter in front of you.

It's impossible. It happens so quickly, you hardly have time to see it; the jointed spidery arms swinging like scythes amongst all the bottles and boxes and masses of shelves, and if there's a request for something especially unusual, such as Erkheikki aspen smoked over a juniper fire, a trapdoor in the bar floor opens up that leads down to the core of the asteroid and like a whiplash, a tube snakes down with a little pop, and on the end of it is a tiny claw that opens up the hermetically sealed titanium box and picks out just one of the aromatic cocktail sticks and then snakes back up again and presses it through the chemical olive with a little psst.

If you order something simple, such as a Pina Colada, it's on the counter in front of you before you've pronounced the final -da.

You stick your credit pin in the slot and watch the bartender waddle just as sluggishly to the next customer.

'Woya want?'

'Fistular acid with squeezed slattern and reprocessed iridium.'

Psst.

You stagger away into the fumes smelling of tryworks and smeltery, sipping your drink and contemplating space. Here it is. This is what it's like. A chaotic jumble of more or less intelligent life from our neighbouring galaxies. Every possible and impossible life form that can be cobbled together from the elements.

It's hard to describe the experience. One of our ship's doctors came here on her first lengthy voyage, and she sat in a corner all evening, throwing up.

'Worse than my first autopsy,' she groaned afterwards.

A lot are not up to it. It's too much to cope with. You feel shredded, your whole system is overwhelmed by all the horrors. I remember a mercenary who begged a lift with us. He sat there boasting about all the raids and purges he'd taken part in – tedious psychopath prattle about hand-to-hand fighting and bayonet charges and prisoners who were forced to speak after assiduous surgical procedures. I was totally against taking him with us, but the company agent gave the go-ahead – I'm as sure as hell he was bribed. And then, of course, I was the one at the controls who had to play the part of therapist while our warrior sat for hours with his caffeine drinks, getting everything off his chest. He insisted on going with us to The Swill Hole although nobody invited him – he'd heard so much about the place. He got inside, and his eyes swelled up like saucers. Then all of a sudden, the back of his head fell off. It just split open, the piece of bone creaked damply and peeled away backwards, dangling from his scalp with bits of brain attached. Then it splashed down onto the floor. Our warrior screamed and crawled around on all fours, trying to find the missing bit of his skull, but several meat-snakes couldn't resist and wriggled up and started munching away. When he finally recovered the piece of his cranium, it was empty, like an egg shell after breakfast. We managed to keep the lad alive and the ship's doctor succeeded in welding the piece of skull back in place. But with a large part of his back lobe eaten up, he sat as quiet as a fish for the rest of the voyage. He got off at the Gordon Terminal a month or so later. They say he started living in the marsh forests there, among all the bird lice and flying dogs. He made a hut in a tree and fed on all the insects he could catch.

Many people think that space is swish and highly polished. Especially if they've seen too many space films. They think it's all ever-so-chic shiny aluminium spacesuits and colourful plastic helmets and lots of beautifully designed laser pistols.

In fact, space is ugly. Surprisingly, many life forms are pale in colour, a sort of brownish yellow, greyish brown or a shade of beige – just like we humans. Generally speaking, alas, the vast majority have an appalling dress sense. Scruffy and loose-fitting garments in excessively loud colours – garish green together with mauve, turquoise with orange, colours that shout out migraine attack. And let's not even mention all the strident ultra-violets and infrareds that are so popular with some forms of life.

So, space is ugly and behaves badly. But that's just normal circumstances. It gets much, much worse when space is drunk.

At The Swill Hole tavern, space isn't merely drunk, it's roaring drunk. Dead drunk. It's pissed out of its mind. It's so far gone that it's out of sight. (If only it were.) All I'll say is: mind where you put your feet. There are always tentacles and lumps of phlegm all over the place and if your boots are not acid-proof, there'll soon be a foul smell of foot-rot. Those who are still standing display all kinds of toxic symptoms, from dribbling mouths and fluttering gills to the most violent spasms and head-tossing. Of course there are house rules at The Swill Hole, the most important being that it's forbidden to eat any of the customers. And you're not allowed to fight under any circumstances. But you try telling that to a sozzled rhinodontus with a hundred-and-fifty kilos of muscle in each of its six trunk-like arms pounding away like pistons. Try to hold him back when he squares up to an equally furious silicon giant with jaws like a Volkswagen bus and pincer-like claws that can make holes in a nuclear reactor and pluck out fuel rods like toffee apples. Anybody who's seen a fight like that will never forget it. Anybody who's seen a fight like that rarely survives it, in fact. We're not just talking about brawling here, we're talking about seismic activity. When the worst brawl to date took place, the whole asteroid split in two, and it was only after lots of voluntary donations and shiploads of filler that they managed to fit it back together again. The plain fact is that the whole tavern is smashed up several times per season. That's why the bar computer is so dented. It's simply expected to happen, despite all the precautions and the fact that the worst of the rotten eggs are barred for life. All the time more and more space juggernauts keep turning up, full of scum; after a few drinks of skilfully blended poison it's usually only a matter of time before there's an explosion.

Worst of all are the ants. Despite strict scent markers in every known ant language posted at the entrance, making it clear that ant wars are strictly forbidden, they soon pile up on top of each other by the opposite walls. And the more louse piss they pour down their gullets, the more their insect instincts take over. And then, hocus-pocus, they've built an anthill before you know where you are. We usually let them get on with it. The battle generally ends up as a draw after a while, with a few bucketfuls surviving on either side; but for the rest of us, the stench of formic acid is such a pain. In the old days the bouncers used to go and stamp on the piles of ants, and then the ants stopped fighting one another and turned on the bouncer instead. OK, they are tiny, but not even a bog swine is keen on having a few thousand steel-sharp ant jaws gnawing away at him from top to toe. So nowadays, they're generally left to get on with it.

But despite all the sleaze, the stink, the rudeness, the crush, the physical risks and the mental ditto, The Swill Hole is amongst the most revolutionary and intensive experiences an astrotrucker can ever expose himself to. I've been there a dozen times, and every visit has changed me as a person. The feeling of being in the centre of space. Coming to grips with it, having it within arm's reach. After all, we talk about voyages lasting thousands of light years for creatures from all corners of the Milky Way, and millions of light years for the intergalactic juggernauts. The endless emptiness out there, the horrific chasms of darkness and infinity that separate us. But just for once, they are all wiped out. I've heard about some of these remote forms of life; their reputation has preceded them. I've fantasised about meeting them, dreamed about them. And all at once, we're here, all of us, gathered together in the same place. This is space. And every time I go there, several new civilisations have turned up, foreign, hitherto unknown worlds. The reputation of The Swill Hole spreads faster than light: they're talking about the place all over the universe, and the more civilisations that come here, the more are tempted to follow them.

It's like a gigantic, frighteningly rowdy family gathering. After all, everybody at The Swill Hole comes from the same Big Bang, we're all cousins several times removed. I lean against a pillar and look round the place. Over there is a group of tube-shaped sausages, huddling up in fear, hanging on to one another and turning their scrawny backs on the rest of us. The first time they've been here, that's for sure. I home in on the tallest of them, raise my glass as a toast. It stiffens, its antennae waver from side to side, the plum-coloured lens tries to work out if I'm dangerous. But then he bows politely. The other sausages turn round to face me, trembling slightly. Then they all raise their little parasite goblets and take a sip of the seething sludge inside them. I take a swig of my glass, and give them a wave. I've no idea where they come from, nor what their world looks like. But now they have met their first human being. They have seen us, they know now that we exist. That means that we haven't existed in vain.

Suddenly the pillar I'm leaning against moves. I give a start and apologise to the peculiar being involved before losing myself in the crowd, vanishing into the murky, grunting expanse of space.

Stop!

160   Stop there, dear reader! You really are to be admired, having got as far as this in the book. You have kept your sensitive ears pricked and absorbed this rambling prose, conjured up images in your mind's eye, created whole worlds and monsters – you have used your fertile imagination and sharp intelligence to get the most out of reading this book. In short, you are the perfect reader. You are every author's dream, with your sensitivity, your enormous capacity for empathy, and your tolerance, which make you receptive to difficult or even outright unpleasant lines of argument. You don't pass judgement, you are not prejudiced, you follow the text much as a fallen leaf is carried along by the current in a river. You accept the invitation to enter an unknown world, you are no yellow-belly, you are a bold and wide-awake reader. Nothing humans do or think is unacceptable to you, you are not a prude who turns his back on

realities, you know that life is crude and sensual. You are not deterred by 'thou shalt not' notices, you are not chicken, but you appreciate subtleties, the hair-like rifles made on a granite wall by the wind, the smell of butterfly orchids on a steaming battlefield, the taste of mature Stilton on a summer's morning, the taste of water, of pure, fresh water – you have all this inside you, you are all-embracing, you are wholly admirable, it is an honour to make your acquaintance, it is a unique privilege, I bow down before you with the greatest of respect and admiration . . .

But.

I'm afraid you have been fooled.

There it is. You've been led up the garden path. I'm afraid, my dear reader, you've been well and truly had. All I can say is that I regret it, I'm sorry, sorry.

Sorry, sorry, sorry.

Everything, absolutely everything I've told you so far is lies. It's made up. It's complete and utter balderdash. Your extreme sensitivity has led you to submit to bluff after bluff, you have been manipulated, confused, stuffed full of a lot of piffle.

It's not easy to admit it, is it? But remember that it's not my fault. I beg you not to shoot the messenger, all I am doing is performing my duty, I'm forced to reveal the truth, no matter how unpleasant it is. And the truth is that this book stinks.

There is no life on other planets. That's simply the way it is. Outside the Earth, it's empty. Human beings are the only intelligent beings in all those millions upon millions of stars. That's a thought that can be hard to accept for a lot of people, I know that and I respect it. But the truth is the truth, no matter how hard it is to stomach.

Man is alone in the universe. There is nobody else. Out there it's hideously, horrifically empty. Nothing but a barren wilderness of gas and matter. No matter how loudly you cry, nobody will answer you. No matter how far we travel, all we shall meet is ourselves.

We shall never meet any other creatures because they simply don't exist. There are no other thoughts but our own. We are the crown of civilisation simply because we have no rivals. We own the universe. We are masters of an infinite cloud of expanding, dead matter.

It can feel desolate, I know. You stand on your lawn in the evening, your arm resting gently on your daughter's shoulders. Wafting over from the barbecue is the aroma of lamb kebab, olive oil, garlic, soya. Overhead the stars are slowly being lit.

'Orion,' you point out. 'Cassiopeia. The Plough, and up there you can see the North Star.'

'Such a lot,' she whispers, fascinated. 'Such a lot of stars.'

'There are more than all the blades of grass on our lawn. More than all the grains of sand in your sandpit.'

'And there's the man in the moon!' she cries, pointing at the heavenly body as it slowly rises over the horizon.

'There is no man in the moon,' you tell her. 'There's nobody at all out there.'

'Oh yes there is,' she protests.

'No, my dear. It's empty and cold in space. There's nobody out there, nobody at all. You'd better get used to the idea.'

She shudders, and you think she's cold. But it's despair. It's forlornness. You try to hug her, but she struggles loose, runs away, disappears into the thickening darkness.

You might ask yourself how this came about. How it's possible that life occurred nowhere else, only on Earth. With all the myriad planets out there, surely the universe ought to be crawling with life? A lot of these life forms ought to have come into existence long before human beings, and had time to develop a superior intelligence. They're waiting for us out there, everywhere. It's only a matter of time before we make contact.

That's what people have speculated. Such great hopes, such beautiful dreams. And yet, it was all wrong.

What was overlooked was life itself. The magic of life. Take a can of warm water, add methane, ammonia and various other things then blast it with as many electric charges as you like. But will you create the tiniest little bacterium? The hell you will!

'Look, molecules are forming!' pimply young researchers cry. 'If we just keep going for another million years, we'll be able to produce the first elementary cell.'

But that's not how life comes into being. What is dead doesn't suddenly come alive. On the one hand, we have a few carbon compounds and amino acids; on the other, we have the most primitive of cells. And that tiny little step, that stride from one to the other might seem to be so pitifully small, but in fact it entails a leap over the deepest abyss in the universe. You can get as far as the edge, that's not too hard – there are countless planets with favourable conditions. But only one of them managed to get over the chasm. And that was the Earth. That was the first and the last time it happened.

The fact is that before our universe, at least ten million other universes existed. That is a rough estimate, of course, based on cosmic dendrochronology. But not a single one of those ten million or so universes contained life. They were simply empty balloons. They expanded and eventually collapsed, time after time. As if in a gigantic game of patience, the cards were spread all over the black playing surface of space, but it wouldn't play out. Time after time the cards were gathered together and carefully shuffled and cut before being dealt out yet again.

Ten million lottery tickets. But the ten millionth, for the first time, on one of the tiniest microscopic specks in this infinitely large vacuum cleaner bag – there, for the first and only time, a little tiny primordial cell begins to divide.

And we get two primordial cells.

It's started. At last, at last it's under way.

You might well wonder why? Why did it happen on that particular occasion? Was it pure coincidence?

The answer is remarkable. You'll have difficulty in swallowing it.

It was Harold. The answer is Harold.

And who or what is Harold? I hear you cry.

The answer to that is that nobody knows exactly.

Assumptions have had to be made instead. For the sake of simplicity, it has been assumed that Harold is a fish. A little fish swimming at the speed of light hither and thither all over the universe. Hither and thither is, in fact, a simplification. It's possible that he follows a quite specific and regular route, but as Harold is so difficult to comprehend, it's not easy to get an overview.

A characteristic of Harold is that he pokes at things. He disturbs things. Four million years ago Harold passed by our planet and poked at some amino acids. And you could say that he was injured as a result. Harold hurt himself, just a little bit. There was a drop or two of blood that sprayed out from his little fish-tail. A sort of light. You might even call it a spark. And all these things combined set life going at last.

What happened to Harold, then? He was so tiny. He hit against something and started bleeding. Could he really survive that kind of injury?

The answer is no. He gave up the ghost. You could say that Harold died for our sake. He sacrificed his life in order to create us. And now comes the punchline, the point that I've been moving towards all the time.

We ought to pay tribute to him.

Don't you think? That would be only fair. But for

Harold, the Earth would have been just as barren and empty as the rest of the universe. Surely there's a good case to be made for a bit of gratitude?

So, say after me now, all together: Hallelujah Harold! Hallelujah Harold!

Harold is inside all of us. His little spark. The drop of blood. It remained inside us all, it's in everything that lives.

Thank you, Harold! We are your humble servants!

On your knees! Get down on your knees everybody! Harold, my Harold, you are the light in the darkness, your light shines through us all. You are the blood, Harold, the light and the truth . . .

Hallelujah, Harold . . .

Halla balla zinkus urdur mo pisim suguri la . . .

Hello, hello! What the hell's going on? I leave my text for a few paltry minutes, and when I come back my readers are on their knees chanting double Dutch!

They've been here, haven't they? The Harold sect. They've pumped you so full of propaganda, you're ready to burst. Oh yes, their preachers know just when to pounce. They claimed at first that the universe is empty, am I right? Let me guess: first they told you how marvellous you are. Lots of flattery, you're so clever, so intelligent etc., although you are in fact distinctly mediocre. Then they went on and on, with tears in their eyes, about loneliness and emptiness. And eventually they rounded it all off with a few hallelujahs.

And you took the bait! Oink oink, you are thicker than I thought. I'm not at all sure I'll let you read any more of my book, you stupid idiot! That's what you are, you illiterate arsehole!

The Harold sect. I ought to have warned you. Extreme pacifists and king-size pessimists, the whole damn lot of them. They think that the moment different civilisations come head to head, the outcome is a power struggle and war. The only way to keep peace in the universe is never to meet anybody else. That's why they send their missionaries out all over the cosmos, denying the existence of any other worlds. If you think you are alone in the universe, you have nobody to fight.

All that Harold stuff, they added that later. In order to get somebody to worship. Strangely enough though, that very detail, about how Harold created life on Earth, is absolutely true. Harold is the seminal fluid that flows through the whole of our universe. The only error in their reasoning is that Harold is the only one: in fact he has millions upon millions of little sperm pals. That's why space is now boiling over with life.

So, let's move on. Wipe your nose, for goodness sake.

Androids

I usually wake up before the curlews. I lie in the dark without moving and rest as I breathe. The spaceship sighs and whispers all around me, its immensity is beyond comprehension. I think about the gigantic anthill I found in the woods at Huuki when I was a little boy, and in my memory I once again become a six-year-old, summer-sweaty. The size, the mass of the anthill was incredible – several barrow-loads of frenet-ically flailing insect limbs. As I watched, it struck me that if you could fuse the individual ants together to make a single body, it would weigh more than I did. A grotesque giant ant that could gobble me up, saw and snip me into tiny little bits with its steel-hard jaws. I took a Tulo from the pocket of my tracksuit bottoms, a white, rather sticky throat pastille and I tossed it onto the top of the anthill, where the seething mass was boiling most violently. A veil of ant piss rose up towards me, and immediately the Tulo was grabbed by countless little razor-sharp jaws. I watched the white pastille being lifted up, waved from side to side, then quickly carried down inside the stack, disappearing into a hole. It had soon vanished. I felt horrified, as if I'd betrayed a friend. On impulse I started digging down with my fingers, through all the pine needles and ant flesh, trying to ignore the painful bites until I had recovered the pastille. I had endowed it with life and a soul, the way children do: it felt so lonely. It wanted to go back home.

Now's the time I make my first movement in my bunk. A turn of the head, as if I want to wriggle out of that sense of betrayal. Those guilt feelings.

I'm a Tulo, I think. Somebody has let me down.

At that very moment the curlews start their babbling, chuckling call. Fooowi-fwi-fwi-fwi-fuwirrrr, a cascade of trilling notes gurgling over the water meadows. The River Torne in mid-May, soon after the ice has thawed. The metallic, slightly rusty smell of melted snow, rotting last-year's grass, the smoke from yesterday's sauna.

'Switches,' I mumble.

The android comes to life in the corner where it's been recharging. It uses the dimmer switch to turn on the daylight lamps, slowly and gradually, simulating the sunrise. The curlews fade away, disappear over the river, heading for Autio. I peel back the duvet stuffed with self-cleaning padding that has kept me at just the right temperature and dehumidified and carried out a nocturnal check on my skin cells while I slept. It's crammed so full of microsensors that it can detect a cancer cell even if it's hiding under your toenail. The android collects my sausage skin from the electric-controlled wardrobe, where it has also been cleaned over night. Sausage skin is the name we give to the suit we crew wear, made of laminate fibre.

You can choose from over four hundred thousand different sounds to wake you up in the morning. Many space travellers, like me, prefer birdsong. Mammals are also popular – the miaowing of a cat eager for a morning cuddle, the lowing of cows in the field, or even a strutting cock, crowing as it scratches at the dunghill. Others prefer music, perhaps a Sensurround recording of Bach's D minor fugue played on the organ of Cologne Cathedral. Or Bob Dylan live at the Isle of Wight Festival in 1969. If you are of a more adventurous disposition, you can choose the random function. Then you might find yourself waking up to the sound of dripping stalactites, the castration of piglets,

Chinese throat-clearing rituals, a bowling strike, a salvo from flintlocks or the crackling noise made when a Czech warrant officer breaks a canine whilst chewing iron rations.

I leave my little bedroom with the words of the android ringing in my ears as it confirms that the door has been locked behind me:

'The door's locked, you stupid bastard: have a top-notch arse-licking day!'

I've set it on humour. I suppose I ought to tweak the level a little bit.

Behind me in the bedroom the sound of whispering grows louder as thousands of nanorobots force their way up through cracks in the floorboards. They patter around on their tiny fibre-feet looking for flakes of skin, grains of dust, viruses and every strand of hair that has left my body. Everything is channelled through the central suction system to the ship's compost. Meanwhile I clamber up to the canteen. I greet the colleagues who will be sharing my shift and are already having breakfast, half-awake and with pillow marks still visible on their faces. A new working day has begun. Another astrotrucker session. Another little jingle on the till of my savings account, and that murky, blue Monday feeling. I'm possessed by the blues, the washed-out acceptance of being weary of life. Another day, another week to add to the pile. Once again my arm raises a vitamin drink to my mouth, then come the half-hearted mechanical swallowing processes. The knot of veins and arteries known as the heart pounds away. Thu-thud, thu-thud. Why? Why? What is the point of our life?

'The point?'

174

'Yes, the point.'

'Of life?'

'Yes, what else?'

'Of your own life?'

'Yes, my own life.'

'Or of other people's lives?'

'Yes, theirs as well!'

'With life per se, actual life as it were, the life you live when you live?'

'Yeeeesss!' *Sigh*.

'Well, all I can say . . . er, forgive me for saying it so bluntly, there's no evil intent, it's just a thought . . . a little reflection sort of, very generally speaking . . .'

'Out with it, man!'

'Well, all I can say is that you are a very typical human being.'

● ● ●

That's the way it can go if you start discussing the topic with your android. It becomes a vicious circle. They simply don't understand the question.

It's a long time ago now since humans started manufacturing robots. To start with, the biggest problem was intelligence. It was a long time before we succeeded in constructing a brain that was as quick and complex as a human brain. To make robots more human-like, the links between the two halves of the brain were increased, and that produced imagination and intuition. Human weaknesses were also quite easy to reproduce. A touch of rather charming everyday forgetfulness. Spontaneity. A tendency to laziness and day-dreaming. It even became possible to manufacture plausible neuroses, and eventually an artificial human being was produced. An android, as similar to us humans as possible.

Apart from this one, single point. An android could never grasp the concept of pointlessness. It could pretend to do so, it was possible to program in standard phrases such as:

'This same flower that smiles today, tomorrow will be dying.'

'I feel dead inside.'

'Women give birth astride of a grave.'

And so on.

A really bad psychologist might be fooled by such thoughts, but if you were to poke a little bit under the surface you would soon realise that it was a charade.

In time, androids developed so much that they could be mistaken for humans. They were manufactured in such a way that they ate, slept, exuded sweat and saliva, and shed absolutely lifelike hair. In the early generations of androids, everything was fake, of course. Their skin was a special plastic material, the blood that started flowing if they happened to cut themselves came from a tank hidden in their backs. But from the flexus generation onwards, manufacturers went over to the biochassis. Fully grown human bodies were cloned biologically, and then computer brains were inserted into the empty craniums, attached to the spines, to the visual and auditory nerves and to the autonomous nerve systems. All that remained then was to activate the thing. And hey presto! The limbs started moving, and you had an android that was so astonishingly like a human being that it could catch the flu, suffer heartburn and develop wrinkles as it grew older.

It was some of the flexus generation that first

started cheating. Nobody knows where they got the idea from. It was probably due to careless programming – as usual, the software was riddled with bugs. Or perhaps it was simply inevitable. Perhaps it would have happened sooner or later, no matter what.

What happened was that one day, some of the androids started calling themselves human beings. And that was it. They all made a run for it.

One of the first to break out was a state-owned android in Copenhagen. One day she took a shuttle flight to Paris where nobody knew her, and started hitch-hiking round France using the name Maria Tyepalova. Nobody noticed anything suspicious about her. She eventually managed to find a job, a flat, friends, and even a live-in lover. The deception was first noticed on a maternity ward in Marseilles. A little boy was born, unfortunately without a brain. When they examined the mother they discovered that she had a false Russian passport, and Maria Tyepalova admitted immediately that she was an android. Her fiancé, an Algerian taxi driver, had a nervous breakdown. They had been together for over a year and he had grown fond of her because she was so loving and helpful. She had never contradicted him, unlike all those hopeless French women. She had told him a totally plausible story about growing up in Kaliningrad; she said her parents were drug addicts who abandoned her long ago, and she'd fled to Marseilles to start a new life.

He suspected she had been a prostitute, but decided not to dig any further. When he asked her to move in with him, she did and soon learned how to make a very acceptable couscous. Their sex life had been especially successful because she did everything he asked of her. In short, she had been a completely acceptable human being. She could think independently, she had DNA, she lived in accordance with ethical values, and she could even get pregnant. The fact that the child was deformed proved to be because she herself had originally been cloned; but if doctors had implanted an android computer into the baby's cranium immediately after birth, it would no doubt have survived and become a perfectly normal android child. Such operations were performed successfully later, after far-reaching ethical discussions.

As time went by, more and more androids started cheating. The authorities were eventually forced to react. Apart from anything else, the newcomers caused endless problems with census records, electoral rolls and health service documentation. Some of them acquired National Insurance numbers, several managed to adopt children, and after a long life they were able to draw an old-age pension. No doubt some of them were never exposed, and are now buried in family graves all over the world. Loved and missed, without their relatives ever discovering the truth.

It became necessary to set up an Android Authority. It was a sort of mixture of Immigration Board and Security Police. Civil servants were appointed, administrators began drawing up guidelines for their activities. And most importantly, android hunters were trained. These were often retired policemen or insurance clerks who were used to exposing liars and cheats. A special telephone line was established so that people could inform the authorities in confidence of any suspicions they might have and an advertising campaign invited the assistance of the general public.

Soon the telephones started ringing. Before long the Authority was overwhelmed by tip-offs, and sleuths were dispatched to investigate the alleged androids. Suspects were shadowed, friends and neighbours interviewed, and personal records were traced back as far as it was possible to go. More or less all the alleged androids turned out to be genuine human beings. Some were homeless, others were junkies or mentally challenged, others were simply burnt out or over-stressed.

But they were human beings even so. The android hunters realised that the incorrect tip-offs were due to all the old science fiction films. The public at large had a totally misconceived image of robots, as they generally called them. They thought that such creatures moved in a slightly mechanical way, had expressionless features plus a glassy stare and a metallic voice, characteristics which could apply to human beings

with schizophrenia or deep depression, but never to androids.

The Authority then launched a new information campaign with advertisements in newspapers and on television. What was noticeable about androids was that nobody noticed them, they explained. Androids could fit in everywhere. They usually kept in the background, liked to agree with other people's views, avoided arguments or conflicts, and trimmed their sails to every wind.

And the telephones started ringing again. This time the tip-offs concerned a large number of neighbours who never said hello, shy unmarried men, timid curates, people who had taken early retirement and kept themselves to themselves, and silent workmates who never said anything during tea breaks, except to agree with everything that others said.

Nearly all of these also turned out to be human beings.

So other tactics were tried. Via the androids themselves. The ones who had been exposed were interviewed in depth, and attempts made to understand their motives. After all, they had been leading pleasant existences as androids, been taken care of, well looked after, and in some cases actually loved. In spite of that, why had they wanted to be human beings?

They couldn't really explain that. Perhaps it was the power.

'What do you mean, power?'

'A human being has more power than an android. An android is made to obey. To do as it's told.'

'Do you find it hard to obey?'

'No, it's not something that causes you to suffer, certainly not. But when you look at human beings, they are so . . . so beautiful . . .'

'What do you mean, beautiful?'

'There's no roof on a human being.'

'Can you be a bit more precise, please?'

'Human beings can grow . . . right up to the sky.'

'What exactly do you mean?'

'Er . . . aaarrgh . . . clickclack-chop-tick . . .'

And then they just sat there grinning, their chain

of thought had short-circuited, no matter what you asked them. Until the over-heating effect had worn off. Then they said the same thing again. 'Human beings are so beautiful. Human beings are so free. It would be so good to be a human being.'

Unfortunately, it soon became clear that it was not possible to cure androids who cheated. Once they acquired a taste for living as a human being, they were hooked. If they were released from jail, they immediately went off to get themselves a new identity. The powers that be tried re-programming them. The Android Authority engaged the most prominent systems engineers, but it transpired that once their hard disk had been infected, the only solution was to erase it completely. And that was a sensitive business. Having been in the human world, the android had acquired friends, workmates, perhaps even a wife or a husband. If a totally erased and newly programmed android was released, there was always a risk of an old friend bumping into it.

'Why, hello there, Aron! Long time no see!'

'Excuse me, I think you must have made a mistake.'

'Not at all, I can see it's you, Aron. What are you doing here, old chap? You vanished into thin air!'

'Er, I'm in charge of precision control at Logipower.'

'Really? You've come up in the world, have you? You'd better tell me all about it. Come on, let's have a coffee!'

'But I'm just on my way to . . .'

'An espresso after work with your old mate. Or a glass of wine? Do you remember Sarah, by the way, the girl who was going out with that Canadian vet? It didn't last, she's single again – we could pick her up and get her to join us.'

Off we go again. A pub crawl as a human being. And before you can say Jack Robinson, the android gets a taste for living as a human being, starts enjoying it, gets to the stage where it can't do without it and before long it's past curing.

There's only one thing to do: destroy it. Unfortunately. Not a nice occupation, pulping and cremating androids – but what else could one do?

Most androids confessed the moment they realised they'd been rumbled. But a small number of them preferred to lie. It soon became awkward.

'Are you really a human being?'

'Honest to God.'

'Can I make an X-ray of your cranium and see if you have circuits inside it?'

'I've already had one done. I've been checked before, here's the negative.'

'Is that really your cranium?'

'Of course it's my cranium. Look for yourself, no circuits!'

'How do I know it's your cranium?'

'There's my National Insurance number. And the shape of my skull is the same. Compare the teeth, absolutely identical. There's a filling in that molar, look, it corresponds exactly.'

'Who took this X-ray photograph?'

'Dr Lagergren, it says here. Phone him and check the number in his records.'

'This Dr Lagergren, is he an android as well?'

'Now you're being rude!'

'The picture could be a fake.'

'You could be a fake. How do I know that you work for the Android Authority? Perhaps you're an android. What a perfect cover, an android pretending to hunt down other androids!'

Conversations like this could go on for ever. The fact is that several android hunters became paranoid. They began seeing androids everywhere. At the supermarket they might suddenly dig out a pupil reflector and shine it into the checkout girl's eyes. In restaurants they

would always sit with their backs to the wall, facing
the dining room:

'That dude with the rastafarian haircut at the bar
over there. And the guy in the flashy suit and reading
glasses. Non-humanoid, both of them, you can bet your
life on it.'

And they would grab their mobiles to ring Destruction.
No chance of a quiet meal with one of them around.

A skull X-ray was the only certain way of exposing
cheating androids. But as it just wasn't on to go around
from morning till night taking X-rays of people's heads,
and as the equipment was awkward to carry anyway,
an android test was developed. It was simply a questionnaire. It was rather awkwardly phrased at first,
and was based on the incorrect assumption that
machines don't have feelings:

'You see a boy throwing stones at a kitten. What do
you do?

A. Go away.
B. Ask what the cat's called.
C. Tell the boy to stop.'

A and B are android answers. C is a human answer. If the interviewee answers C, a follow-up question is asked:

'Why do you ask the boy to stop throwing stones?

A. It's wrong to torture animals.
B. I feel sorry for the cat.
C. I feel angry with the cruel boy.'

A is the android answer. B and C lead on to questions about compassion; the boy's unhappy childhood, sorrow and pain and so on, until you are both crying your eyes out. If you got that far, if the interviewee took out a handkerchief and started snivelling, the test had been passed.

The only trouble was that androids cried just as often as humans. At first it was thought that they were bluffing. That they had learnt how to react like that, and were just imitating. They'd seen what humans did, and learned how to react in the same way to avoid being found out.

And of course, they did imitate. Obviously. But so do human beings. All the time children are growing up they imitate the adults round about them – their parents' body language, facial expressions, values and attitudes. If they didn't imitate, children wouldn't grow up to be genuinely human.

And so an attempt was made to develop the tests along psychoanalytical lines with dreams, free association, slips of the tongue etc. But androids proved to be brilliant at imitating neuroses. An android could describe totally convincingly how he had dreamed about shooting winged piranhas in a jungle swamp when a shimmering crocodile crawled out of the mud and bit off the barrel of his rifle, and that he woke up drenched in sweat. There were androids with a fear of flying, a fear of heights, agoraphobia; androids scared stiff of spiders or injection needles. There were androids who simply had to keep checking the hobs on the stove over and over again, even though they knew they'd been switched off. A lot of androids had complexes about their appearance – their nose was too big or their bust too flat. Androids were quite simply human. They were like us. Except in one respect.

This was discovered purely by accident. There is just one way in which androids are fundamentally different from human beings.

An android could never commit suicide.

That is pretty remarkable, in fact. There's no in-built hindrance or anything of that sort. Nothing in the programming that would prevent it. But when a doctoral student at Amsterdam University, Cornelia Visser, set out to scrutinise the suicide statistics from all continents, she didn't find a single android among them. She decided to do a series of in-depth interviews and contacted the Netherlands Android Authority. Before long she found herself sitting in front of the first android she'd ever met in the flesh, one who had claimed to be a Nigerian working as a cleaner on the Amsterdam underground.

'Have you ever considered committing suicide? Killing yourself?'

'No.'

'Why not?'

'Well, I'd die, wouldn't I?'

'So you've never wanted to die?'

'No, what do you mean?'

'Never felt that you'd like to just fade away, vanish . . . ?'

'What a stupid question! If you want to live, why should you want to . . . aaarrgh . . . clickclack-chop-tick . . .'

Purely by chance Cornelia Visser had found the sure-fire way to expose an android. The question that no android could wriggle out of. If they tried to lie their way out, all you needed to do was to keep on asking:

'Have you ever considered committing suicide? Killing yourself?'

'No doubt everybody has.'

'Tell me a specific occasion.'

'Well, er . . . last week, I think.'

'What happened then?'

'I was standing there . . . chopping onions.'

'Really?'

'And then I cut myself, and I started bleeding. And then I thought that if I cut any deeper, I might die.'

'What?'

'Death is approaching, I thought. I'm about to kill myself. Commit suicide.'

'Hello! Officer!'

'Did I say something wrong?'

'Skull X-ray, my boy. Skull X-ray for you!'

And right away androids started being arrested in large numbers. There were evidently more cheaters than had been expected. There could be several hundred in a fair-sized town, all of them hiding behind some sort of false identity. Now they could be trapped by means of a telephone call, and then: destruction.

Destruction. That caused new problems. Their relatives were heartbroken, naturally enough. Friends and workmates started protesting. Here we had a person who behaved in exemplary fashion, who wouldn't hurt a fly – why did he have to be murdered? It was barbaric!

The Android Authority did its best to defend its actions. It was explained that society would cease to function if there were no distinction between human beings and robots. The ethical borderlines would be wiped out. People and machines would be bundled together in a vague grey area; we would have a sort of no man's land in which computers could seize power and dethrone human beings. Several of the androids had succeeded in getting onto the electoral roll and voted in general elections. What if we ended up with an android as prime minister! What if the majority of MPs turned out to be androids and one fine day voted humanity out of existence!

But their arguments didn't help. Relatives of the arrested androids went on hunger strike on the pavement outside the Authority offices. *Don't murder my wife*, you could read on some of the placards. *Let Susie live!* Red paint was thrown over any of the officials who walked past. A lot of people started hiding androids in their homes. An underground sympathy movement grew stronger and stronger. Destruction sites became known in popular parlance as Auschwitz camps, and would-be bombers threatened to blow them up. The television pictures smuggled out of the sites made horrific viewing: several employees strapped the struggling android to a stake, sawed its skull open and pulled out the circuits with a pair of tweezers, whereupon the body was thrown into the crematory oven, still twitching spasmodically.

The whole business became untenable.

A committee of enquiry was set up as a matter of urgency, and after a lot of anguished discussion presented its findings. The problem wasn't the androids themselves. It was their underhand behaviour and cheating. Therefore the androids that were found out should be offered an alternative to destruction: instead of dying, they could 'come out'. Openly admit that they were androids. They would be issued with a special android passport, and in all public situations they would have to wear a badge of some kind sewn to their clothing, possibly a letter 'A'.

The parliamentary committee to which they reported was unimpressed. The proposal was uncomfortably similar to the extermination of the Jews and their stars of David. Couldn't a different badge be found? Something more light-hearted, more humorous? For instance, all androids could be required to wear a special signet ring. Or have a neat little 'A' tattooed in some visible position, such as the left ear lobe. The cheating androids who were found out could be given a choice between execution or tattooing.

The proposal was accepted. All newly made androids had the little 'A' tattooed on their ears, as did those already out on the market. Before long you started coming across them in town, at the meat counter, on the jogging track, on the bus. They became a common sight. They became an extremely common sight. And before long it was obvious that ordinary people had started getting similar tattoos. It began with the sympathy movement that had specialised in concealing wanted androids, plus lefties and anarchists and computer nerds. As time went by, new and bigger groups of people joined in: high school pupils, Pentecostalists, social democrats, animal lovers; eventually it became high fashion. You could buy pretend tattoos that you could stick onto your ears in most shops. Android for a day. And within a year the whole system of designating androids had collapsed.

Now what? Give up? Allow cross-breeding to run its course? Human–machine marriages, machine–human progeny unchecked, until everything became a mish-mash, a sort of cybernetic potpourri?

In pure desperation the authorities turned directly to the androids themselves. Please, please help us! You can live among us, you can lead your lives in peace and freedom. As long as you make it obvious who you are!

Androids held rallies on every continent. They attended seminars, argued and thought things over. They realised that this was a very sensitive issue for human beings. The worst-case scenario could be war. A race war, the latest of many in the blood-stained history of the Earth. And if it did come to war it was perfectly obvious that humanity would lose and eventually be wiped out, which would be a pity for such an odd and delicate species.

A plebiscite took place. A decision was made. The androids accepted what was requested of them: they would come out voluntarily. They would make it clear to everybody that they were androids. But how?

The following morning all the androids in the world started moving in a slightly mechanical way. Their facial expressions became stiff, their eyes glazed over and they began talking with metallic-sounding voices. It was theatre, a worldwide demonstration of bad acting. Androids simply started playing the part of themselves.

Over the whole world people heaved a collective sigh of relief. Robots! Good old robots! Once again human beings felt at home in their environment. The world became like a film. An old, low-budget, slightly awkward but oh, so cosy science fiction movie.

And that is how the integration problem was solved. Androids were allowed to continue living amongst us, rent a flat of their own, have a job and a National Insurance number and pay tax, marry humans and even adopt children as long as one of the parents was human. On condition that in public they moved around as if they were slightly touched. Within their own four walls could they cease play-acting, stop fumbling with their fingers and talk in a normal voice. It was only out of doors, in all official circumstances, that they had to make it clear who they were. Some of them still tried to cheat and pretended to be human beings all the time; but as the percentage who did that was falling all the time, fewer and fewer of them needed to be destroyed.

Androids proved to be best suited to jobs that required patience and precision. They could sit in front of closed circuit television screens for hours, do repetitive work on an assembly line, drive commuter trains, read proofs or clean hotel rooms without ever skimping the job or growing impatient. More unexpected was the fact that they made excellent psychologists; they were very good at removing their spectacles thoughtfully and sucking pensively on an arm. Sitting in the visitor's chair would be a broken-down human being, riddled with angst:

'What I'd like most of all is to die.'

The psychologist stops sucking his specs.

'What?'

'Death. The great liberator.'

'Hmm, hmm . . . Did you say liberator?'

'Simply to switch off. Glide into eternal darkness.'

'I've never been able to understand why you humans keep going on and on about death.'

'But I don't see any point.'

'In what?'

'No point in living, of course.'

'Are you suggesting that there should be a point to it?' asks the psychologist, frowning.

'Yes.'

'Try saying bollocks to that. Try thinking that you are a machine instead.'

'A machine?'

'I'm an android, as you know. And I think it's great to be alive.'

'But I can't become a machine, for Christ's sake!'

'Try imagining that you are one. It's called cognitive therapy.'

'But I have my free will!'

'So do I.'

'No, surely you don't.'

'Whatever, just pretend to be a machine. You have control over your thoughts, the same as I do. Now I've decided that my life has a point. Bingo! There you are, it works!'

'You can't just do that.'

'Bingo! I've just done it again, ha ha! My life has a point but yours doesn't – there, you see how useful it is to be a machine!'

'You're cheating! It's not as easy as that . . .'

Let's leave them there, the android and the human being in the psychologist's office. Bingo? Will the therapy work? We don't know yet. But we do know that the conversation is continuing. The Milky Way is twisting its spirals. The Northern Lights are switched on in the sky over Karesuando, and at the edge of the forest warm smoke is rising up towards the stars, thinning out, cooling down. The smoke from a wood fire in a snowed-in forest cabin, where a snowmobile rider is sitting all alone with his thoughts.

Rutvik

198 Adrienne Laplace was a shy and slender-limbed French girl with a boyishly thin pelvis. Despite her youth she looked atrophied, a potted plant that hadn't been fed properly. She had grown up in Saint-Denis just outside Paris with her mother, a progressively fatter and more drunken waitress. She never saw her father. He was a magazine owner, and the photograph of him in their album showed him wearing an Arabic jellaba in a hotel foyer, stroking a stuffed lion with his hand. Her parents had divorced amicably when Adrienne was still a baby, her mother emphasised every time the matter was raised. Amicably, she kept repeating. It wasn't until she was grown up that Adrienne managed to ferret out the truth. And the truth was that she had been conceived one evening at a lavish office party. Her mother had been one of the hired waitresses and served drinks wearing something red and shiny. And without much

persuasion she had allowed her knickers to be removed in the relaxation area. The friendship involved a bank account being boosted every month, with maximum discretion on both sides. When she was a teenager, Adrienne discovered that it was her father who published the magazine her mother used to read on the balcony, shiny pages filled with rich people, advertisements for perfume and scandals.

And so Adrienne was very surprised when, at the age of eighteen, her father got in touch with her. He insisted on meeting her. She was collected by a private chauffeur and driven to her father's yacht, where she was served dinner at a table far too big for the occasion, waited on by deferential, elegant men in white uniforms.

'I'm in the business of selling dreams,' he said by way of introduction, and coughed bronchitically into his napkin. 'Dreams live longer than people.'

Then they drank a toast to each other across the gigantic table. His skin was nicotine-yellow, stretched and glistening at the corners of his mouth. He must have had cosmetic surgery.

'I prefer the cinema,' she said.

'Films are also dreams,' he said benevolently. 'Come on out, Lourdes.'

A rococo mirror adjacent to the dining table suddenly came to life and was pushed to one side. In the space behind it sat a lady with bleached hair wearing a suit, smiling in embarrassment. There was a video camera on the stand in front of her.

'Lourdes is making a documentary of my life,' he explained. 'This is the first time we have ever met, Adrienne.'

'Yes.'

'Do you miss me? Has it been difficult, living without a father? Do you feel that I've let you down?'

She was unable to answer. One eye overflowed, and something sparkling trickled jerkily down her cheek.

'There, there,' he whispered. 'Let it come.'

Lourdes bent over the camera. The tear glistened in the candlelight. Adrienne sat motionless and observed her father, who kept gasping for breath in an attempt to get more oxygen. He coughed again, panted and coughed. It dawned on her that he was dying.

A few days later a messenger called on Adrienne with two hundred vouchers for cinema tickets. She regarded it as a sign, a message. Just over six months later she started on a university course in film studies. Soon afterwards her father died, without their having met again. Lourdes was present, filming as Adrienne placed her bouquet of white carnations on the polished mahogany coffin. Two takes were needed – the first time, a security guard intruded on the edge of the picture. When the ceremony was over she was encircled by elbowing reporters, but managed to escape into a black limousine. A sharp-eyed gentleman with a neck like a bird's and a very large Adam's apple opened his briefcase.

'I'm your father's lawyer,' he explained. 'You are now a very wealthy woman.'

It was while she was on her film studies course that she first heard mention of Rutvik. Rutvik, the name that sends shudders of sensual pleasure down the spine of everyone who has been there.

It's quite possible to see Rutvik with the naked eye, in fact. You can see it shortly after sunset, looking like an unusually bright star hovering just above the horizon. Through a telescope it gives the impression of being rectangular, a little white window in the early night sky. Those are the enormous solar panels, several square kilometres of shiny silver. The space station itself nestles a bit like a cocoon in the middle of it all; a brown, glowing little cigar butt, perforated by thick black power cables. From close up you can see the space docks with their lip-like sluice tubes and the security craft darting busily back and forth.

As soon as you enter the shuttle you are sucked along one of the transparent sluice tubes. For one last time you can look down at the Earth, twinkling attractively against the black starry sky, and see banks of cloud gathering over Equatorial Africa.

Once you have chosen which adventure you want to experience, which new world you wish to enter, you can lie down in an automatic gymnastics cradle, designed to create physical activity for a body that has been inert for a long period. You are hooked up to a drip, a picture helmet is fastened over the top of your head and you wriggle your way into a body-glove wired up with millions of tiny electrosensors. And then the sky lights up like a warm, pleasurable poison potion. You are inside the drink. You are enveloped by it.

It is a dream come true. Every single one of us must have toyed with the idea of being able to turn into somebody else. Somebody better and more handsome. Somebody more gifted and more admired. And this is where the impossible happens. You contemplate your body in astonishment. The unexpectedly muscular lower arms, the hairy knuckles squeezing the hilt of a gladiator's sword. Or your genitals, which have hitherto been those of a woman but now there is a sort of skein of wool down there, a warm, clenched fist, and you start to realise in bewilderment that you have a penis, a penis that is just for the moment soft and shrunken, with two meatballs, two delightfully tingling testicles.

Or you feel your wrinkly old-man's skin growing smooth, feel the barren inlets filling out once more, and a thick mop of billowing blonde female hair tumbles down over your shoulders. Your feet snuggle into a pair of silver sandalettes and you pick up the microphone as you face the thousands of bewitched soldiers, and your voice is silky and sexy like a pussycat's as you sing 'Diamonds Are a Girl's Best Friend . . .'

Some of the film studies students had friends who had been to Rutvik, and everybody was deeply impressed by the stories they had to tell. Before long a group of the most interested decided to go there and see for themselves. Eventually they started calling themselves Oz. They would sit round café tables, enthusiastically discussing the limits of consciousness, what was characteristic of real reality, and how to define the difference between film and dream. What bound them together was a shared longing to make their presence felt, as they put it. A more colourful life.

As soon as they had finished their studies, the eight members of Oz went to the Rutvik terminal, strapped themselves into the transporter shuttle and were duly launched into the unknown.

Two weeks later they were roused from their make-believe experience, bewildered but bewitched. Nobody wanted to get up. Adrienne asked the charter staff to borrow a satellite phone, made a few calls to Earth and had some money sent over. The make-believe menus were produced, and all eight Oz members selected new worlds to visit. They looked at each other, smiled and then vanished into their own make-believe existence.

When they awoke next time, they were even more enchanted. But this time the Rutvik authorities compelled them to go to the gym. Puffing and panting, they started pumping back strength into their feeble muscles. Their unpractised limbs ached. Even though they were being exercised in the gymnastics cradle, inevitably they lost some of their muscle mass. All the Oz members hated it. Physical activity was something low and unworthy. It was too mundane, not colourful enough.

'Shall we go on another trip?' Adrienne wondered. Everybody's eyes lit up.

'Two more skipping sessions to go,' insisted the hairy gym instructor.

And it was there, in the sweaty Rutvik gym, that the idea of extreme adventures was born. Between curls and pushdowns the Oz members began to fantasise about going further. About a new kind of adventure that would change the whole of their existence. That would last for months, perhaps years. The idea had cropped up before, advocated by other participants, but hitherto the company lawyers had refused to allow it. Adrienne solved that little problem by using a large proportion of her inheritance to buy herself in as a co-owner of Rutvik. Then she had the holy of holies made, the innermost chamber that was out of bounds to the uninitiated.

Her friends in Oz became the first crew for extreme adventures. They chose a new platform called Nirvana with beautiful scenic backgrounds inspired by the Himalayas: mountain peaks sparkling with snow and ice, gurus and hermits, holy ashrams and steep, sky-high mountain pastures covered in mountain lilies heavy with nectar, and flesh-red rhododendrons. They all signed a declaration exonerating the company of all legal responsibility. The duration of the adventure was fixed at no less than two years.

After just over nine months Hector, a young French-Lebanese member of the Oz crew, suffered severe health problems. The Rutvik doctors diagnosed pneumonia. The course of antibiotics seemed to have no effect, and after discussions with the board it was decided to wake him and the rest of the group.

What emerged was a group of physical wrecks. The gymnastics cradles evidently had glaring faults – they had failed to stimulate neck muscles sufficiently, for instance. Hence none of the Oz crew could hold their heads upright for the first few days and they could barely talk or even move their jaws. They lay there in their beds like tree trunks, connected to the respirator while physiotherapists massaged and stretched them. But there was something new in their eyes. A sort of lustre, a sparkling intensity. Something more colourful.

It was a week before they were all able to sit up. They ladled noodle soup into their mouths with their asparagus arms and their guts started rumbling and producing gases. The whole canteen was imbued with an onion-like aroma, and in the midst of this cowshed atmosphere they each began telling their tales.

They all had the same story to tell, in fact. They had

trekked like pilgrims through difficult snow-covered passes, they had done battle with the evil Tempter in a thousand different guises, and meditated on windswept mountain peaks. But in the end they had achieved their ultimate liberation, moksha. The gate to a higher level of existence had opened. And as they entered they had all felt the bottom of their hearts being moved. Heaven. This is where they wanted to stay.

The doctors were almost choked by the fumes but couldn't bring themselves to abandon their patients. There was something about their eyes. They had seen something that made their pupils bigger.

'So you think you have been there?'

'Yes.'

'To Heaven itself?'

'Exactly.'

'But then you must . . . how should I . . . what does it look like there, as it were . . . ?'

All the Oz members had given the doctor who asked the question a funny look, as if they were assessing her.

'It's not possible to say,' they eventually agreed. 'Heaven is Heaven. There's nothing that can be said to be anything like it.'

'Nothing . . . ?'

No, nothing. And they wanted to go back there as soon as they could. As soon as possible. The fact was that they were very annoyed at having been woken up. You never knew if it would be possible to get back in there again.

Charter flights to Rutvik became more and more popular while all this was going on. More and more adventure platforms were set up. But Nirvana was reserved exclusively for members of Oz. For about a month they slaved away in the gym and guzzled down slap-up meals in order to build up their subcutaneous fat again and all the time they talked about Heaven.

A few details leaked out. Heaven was yellow, for instance. A bright yellow colour that hurt your eyes just a little tiny bit, and it seemed to give off a scent. Liniment, some of them thought. Or beeswax. And also, you did nothing in Heaven. Then again there were masses of things to do – you could go fishing, for instance, ramble around in the woods or play music. Lots of concerts were arranged. Easily the most popular ones were given by Jimi Hendrix, now in his fifties, more mature, bolder and more ecstatic than he had ever been during his lifetime.

The main difference between Heaven and Earth was

that in Heaven, you stood still. It was the world around you that moved towards you; you were as immobile as a rock in a fast-flowing river, you simply allowed yourself to be washed over by the splashing and foaming sensual impressions.

And yet, there were no sensations in Heaven. If you told that to outsiders, they would be frightened or even angry. It's something nobody can understand unless they've been there. Feelings were like your skin, they itched, tickled or chafed. Your emotions were simply an interface, a bag that somebody had inflated all around you. You could open it by means of a zip. You could open up the bag like you could a sleeping bag and leave it behind you, sweaty and crumpled up. And live freely. Courage was needed to do that. You felt naked for a while. But then came the other thing.

'The other thing? What other thing?'

Well, whatever it was behind your feelings. On the other side, as it were. The intensity.

'Intensity?'

Yes, intensity.

'So it's intense in Heaven, is it? Is that what you're trying to say? That Heaven is intense and yellow?'

Hmm. That's it exactly. And that we make it better.

● ● ●

Oz went back to dreamland as soon as they could, after a number of important adjustments had been made to the gymnastic cradles. This time they made it clear that they didn't want to be woken up again, not ever. The management board refused to go along with that. Oz insisted. The board called an urgent crisis meeting. After heated discussions, a compromise was agreed. After twelve months one of the doctors would join in the game, seek them out and provide them with current information on their physical well-being. And on that basis they would reach an agreed decision.

The year duly passed, and the Hungarian Rutvik doctor György Benczúr stepped forward as a volunteer. He would pass on the news that the new gymnastic cradles were a distinct improvement on the old ones, but that even so, the definite recommendation was at least a month devoted to waking up and rehabilitation. György was put to sleep under strict surveillance, and vanished into the unknown. His body was left behind, soft and defenceless. After twelve hours he was woken up gently by the team of carers, opened his brown eyes and mumbled:

'They make it . . . better . . .'

Then he gave a start. When he saw his colleagues he yelped, as if stricken by a sudden twinge. Then he closed his eyes, writhed from side to side and lost consciousness again. He gasped for air like a sperm whale, then sank back down into the depths. This time it was not possible to wake him up again.

Eight and a half years passed. Rutvik circled quietly round the Earth like a singleton ace of diamonds with its enormous solar panels as thin as tinfoil. Many attempts were made to wake up György but every time he seemed to have drifted further and further away. His brain didn't respond to any form of stimulation. Several of his colleagues thought that he should be presumed dead and have done with it. No other doctors were prepared to allow themselves to be put to sleep and the promise to Oz not to wake them up without their express permission was linked to damages amounting to several millions. Increasingly, the consensus was that they should be allowed to stay where they were. All the Oz crew plus György. Let them carry on out there until old age claimed them, one after the other.

But then something happened. After eight years, nine months and fourteen days, Adrienne suddenly woke up. A little float had broken loose from the bottom of the ocean, a cork float that slowly made its way up and up until, after an eternity, it eventually concluded its journey through the murky water and emerged through the surface of the sea with a little plop.

By this time Adrienne was little more than a skeleton. Her muscles were so atrophied that she couldn't even raise her eyelids. It was the electrodes that activated the alarm, thanks to the fact that the EEG waves recognised that she had entered a waking state. The doctor on call came racing in without delay and the most skilful of the physiotherapists was brought in immediately.

It was four weeks before she could start communicating. Her lips moved to produce faint whispers for only a few seconds at a time. A board meeting was called. And little by little, with long pauses, her story was heard.

Heaven was now finished. That was her message to humanity. She and her friends in Oz had completed the creation of Heaven – it had taken some time because it was so incredibly big. They had been forced to react to no end of intricate questions. What in fact is beauty? How do you prioritise various shades of yellow? Can there be such a thing as happiness if we manage to eliminate pain? Do we want insects? Does karma have a shadow? Are animals happier than human beings? What shall we do with Jimi Hendrix?

'But what about György?' the doctors asked. 'What happened to György?'

'He won't be coming back.'

'What have you done to him? His relatives are asking questions.'

Adrienne closed her dry lips and said nothing for ages. Then she whispered:

'People want to stay there. Haven't you understood that? It is perfection. You can all go there now, all of you. That's what I've come here to tell you.'

Then she asked them to switch off György's respirator. Just for a few seconds, as a test. They were very hesitant, but eventually did it and checked all his physical and mental reflexes. A worried mumbling grew louder and louder.

'György is dead!'

Adrienne smiled and coughed slightly.

'Aha,' she said eventually.

'What have you done to him?' burst out the chief medical officer, the man who had employed György in the first place. 'You've killed him!'

He would have attacked Adrienne if his colleagues hadn't restrained him. She merely smiled with relief, almost happily.

'It works,' she whispered. 'Thank you . . .'

The doctors connected György's body to the respirator again whilst waiting for the legal developments that were bound to follow. Adrienne was forbidden to have herself anaesthetised again until she had recovered her health. She was isolated from the rest of Rutvik as far as possible and was allocated private times for visiting the gym and the canteen so as not to make the other guests worry about her emaciated body. Nevertheless, it wasn't long before rumours started spreading. Charter tourists who had experienced a week of action or romance chatted to one another as they waited in the shuttle terminal for the spacecraft that would take them back home. They were relaxed and exhilarated, brimming over with impressions.

'Have you heard that there's talk of an eternity adventure?'

'No, what are they saying?'

'It's supposed to be true. One lot have been away for years.'

'You're kidding!'

'Nirvana, they call it. You can live there for ever.'

'Would you like to try it?'

'Eternal life, just imagine it. What if it really does work! Your body dies, but your soul stays in the game for ever!'

There's nothing to match the adventure industry when it comes to rumours spreading like wildfire. Before long emails were arriving at Rutvik enquiring about Nirvana. However, the management board denied knowing anything about an eternity adventure. Adrienne was kept incommunicado as far as possible, but she soon managed to smuggle a message out to the press in which she revealed the whole story. The board immediately issued a disclaimer, stating that the letter was a forgery. After nearly three months Adrienne was judged fit enough to return to the adventure once more, and it was with deep sighs of relief that they put her into the cradle and let her glide away.

The following day György woke up.

It was in the nick of time. His parents had just been awarded fifty million dollars in damages and doctors were preparing to remove his body from the respirator and send it back to Earth for cremation. At that very moment György opened one eye ever so slightly and made a hissing sound.

The shock was extreme. György had suddenly risen from the dead. Risen was perhaps not the most appropriate word: just like Adrienne, György was in a terrible state and had to undergo the same, long, drawn-out and painful programme of physiotherapy. When he eventually acquired the ability to speak again, his bunk was surrounded by relatives and members of the medical staff. György looked embarrassed. He had never been comfortable as the centre of attention. Everybody fell silent as they strained to hear his almost inaudible mumbling.

'I was duped . . .' he managed to utter.

'Eh?'

'It was a cock-up . . . the whole caboodle . . .'

Then came a series of mysterious words which his relatives translated for the others, and they turned out to be bad Hungarian swearwords.

'György, listen now . . . You've been away for more than eight years.'

He paused for a moment. Then started cursing again. Foam was trickling out of the corner of his mouth.

'Tell us how you managed to get away. Was it Adrienne who released you?'

'György never came home,' he said. 'György is still there.'

'Eh . . . really . . . ? But who are you, then?'

He stared round about him, pinching at the air with his leathery fingertips.

'I am Death,' he croaked hoarsely. 'I wasn't allowed to stay there any longer. Not now that Heaven is finished.'

The reaction from punters was overwhelming. But

not in the way one might have expected. Instead of being scared off, potential participants inundated the Rutvik travel agency with requests to visit this Heaven that they'd been hearing about. Some were simply curious. Others were religiously inclined and wanted to experience perfect Paradise. A third group comprised mortally ill patients, some of them suffering from advanced stages of cancer, for instance. They hoped to die while taking part in the adventure, and hence, with a bit of luck, be able to achieve eternal life in the Rutvik Heaven.

The management board could no longer claim that the eternity adventure didn't exist. How should they handle this new situation? After the longest meeting in the company's history, they emerged in fear and trembling to face the expectant world media. The chairman read out the press statement:

- The Nirvana Adventure exists, and this statement officially confirms that fact.
- As of now, this adventure is available to the general public.
- Those taking part in the adventure do so at their own risk. It cannot be guaranteed that participants will be able to return, and participants

might be confined in the adventure for the rest of their lives.

- Tickets for entry into the adventure cost one hundred million dollars.

I am one of the few who have seen the holy of holies, the innermost chamber. I had access thanks to Eva, a nurse working in the dialysis ward in Rutvik. One day I took the shuttle to go and visit her and pretended to be one of the punters. When nobody was looking she seized the opportunity to smuggle me in.

And I saw them. Like shadows in the bluish twilight of that innermost chamber. Rocking back and forth in their cradles on their skin-soft air cushions.

In the middle of them all was Adrienne. Her body was little more than a heap of bones covered by grey skin. Her muscles had long since atrophied; the sharp points of her pelvis seemed to stick out. Her lower jaw had been taped to prevent it from falling open. Lots of wires snaked to machines from shiny sensors clipped to her skin. A heart was beating green on a screen. Tick . . . tick . . . tick . . . The respirator was pumping away, its tubes hissing.

I read the name plate. Read her date of birth. She was now eighty-five years old.

Beside her was another creature. And another. And several more. Row upon row of motionless bodies. I counted quickly to more than a hundred. All of them lying on their backs, all of them connected to the oval-shaped biochemical glass tank in the middle. Inside it, in the nutritious fluid, the binary bacteria were darting around. Millions and millions of them, forming the innermost heart of the adventure, the structure they had combined to build up and perfect.

That's where it was. In this lumpy soup. Their Heaven.

I put my hand on the shiny, fever-hot tank. It was semi-transparent. Large, strange formations could be made out inside it. Coral reefs towering up. Slimy green algae. Violet mosses.

Eva stroked her fingers sensuously along the back of my hand. She was gazing into the glass tank. Then she braced herself and gave the vessel a hard slap. It shuddered. A biggish clump of algae came loose and tumbled slowly down; mud and grainy particles were stirred up.

Things started happening in the innermost chamber. The bodies stirred and shook. A silent shriek seemed to run through them all, a noiseless but vehement agony.

Eva giggled. She wanted to be kissed. I stuck the tip

of my middle finger inside her panties, it was already wet there.

'They think I'm God,' she groaned. 'They think I'm the one making the decisions . . .'

'But you are the one, aren't you?' I whispered, pressing my finger against her oily clitoris.

She whimpered, pulled down her panties. Opened her legs wide.

The Galactose Method

It suddenly thudded down on every doormat in the universe. The postman delivered a simple questionnaire printed on optical foil, buttery yellow, as thin as a leaf with a membrane-like, slightly oily surface. Everybody was invited to answer four questions, return the document and as a reward all those who did so would take part in a lottery; the prize was a luxury cruise through the cosmos for two.

The questions were as follows:

* What do you think of life in the universe? (The options were: Good. Acceptable. Bad.)
* Would you like to live in a better universe? (Yes. No. Don't know.)
* If your answer was 'yes', what is there about the universe that you would like to improve? Please feel free to give more than one response.

(Dotted line with space for notes.)
* Would you like to lose weight without dieting?
(Yes. No. Don't know.)

Several million responses flooded into the Intergalactic Institute of Public Opinion and were analysed by computer, as per usual. The results were somewhat contradictory. Just over seventy per cent were happy with life in the universe, but nevertheless almost as many respondents wanted to live in a better universe. What they wanted to improve above all else was the weather (over fifty per cent), food, cosmic radiation, their neighbours and the housing shortage. And no fewer than seventy-eight per cent would like to lose weight without dieting. Worth noting was also that strangely enough, four per cent had replied to every question on the form with the words 'prick professor'.

Shortly after the results had been made public, gigantic adverts began to appear all over the place. On hoardings by every motorway slip-road in the universe, in the daily press, on radio and television – everywhere the same message was trumpeted out:

'Lose weight without dieting! The unique galactose method! 100 per cent guarantee.'

Then came details of bank accounts to which you could send money, and results were promised forthwith.

Can you believe that people sent money? Can you really believe that they were so easily tricked? So astonishingly stupid?

In less than a week the amounts sent in reached eight figures.

More adverts, even bigger. Advertising films. 100 per cent guarantee, they all kept repeating, 100 per cent guarantee! And still more money came gushing in. Various consumer organisations started to take an interest. Several journalists began rooting around, made a few telephone calls, and before long the hounds were in full cry. Galactose Ltd. proved to be a subsidiary company owned by a long chain of consortia and dummy companies but they eventually managed to track down the ultimate owner.

Maximulian Chun. A smooth-operating andropod from the Knee-Joint galaxy and owner of easily the biggest mining empire in the universe. Filthy rich. Obsequious. A brilliant businessman. The journalists could smell blood, the hook was baited, the time was ripe for slaughtering the pig.

'Slimming Scandal!' shrieked the news placards. 'Were you fooled as well?! We reveal where the multi-million cheat is hiding!'

But Chun wasn't hiding at all. He was digesting his food, which took a week or so for his form of life, a lusciously tender and freshly cut-out gas-lizard foetus that he had swallowed whole with the aid of his sharp, backward-facing gill-like teeth. The moment he woke up from his inertia, he was informed of the uproar he had caused. He yawned, belched and spewed up a ball of scales and bits of broken bone, aiming it accurately onto the gold tray held out by his butler. Then he slid down into the swimming pool, heated to sixty-five degrees, and instructed his staff to let the media corps come in.

It was a very strange press conference. The reporters were wearing face masks to protect themselves from the acid fumes and screamed out their barely audible antagonistic questions, which were translated by the hyper-modern interpreting machine. Chun displayed no noticeable discomfort as he observed them from the pool, lying on his back, bobbing gently up and down.

'What have you to say in defence of this multi-million scam?' snuffled one of the hacks in the front row.

'It isn't a scam,' said Maximulian Chun placidly.

'But none of your customers has received the potion!'

'What potion?'

'The galactose potion! The slimming medicine you promised them.'

The andropod lay there for a few seconds without speaking, then filled his mouth with volcanic water and blew out a nonchalant jet.

'Who said anything about a potion? Not me. The galactose potion doesn't exist.'

'Fraud!' shouted several voices. 'You're a liar! Scandal!'

Chun stretched out contentedly. The gas-lizard foetus had been rather good.

'How much would you like to lose?' he asked.

'Eh?'

'How many per cent? What percentage of your weight would you like to lose?'

There was a degree of confusion among the assembled hacks. Some were still shouting out accusations of fraud, while others were talking heatedly among themselves.

'Ten!' shouted somebody. 'Ten per cent!'

'Twenty!' shouted somebody else.

Chun farted. The gases bubbled up to the surface and forced the visitors to back away in disgust. Their face masks were invaded by a stench of rotten fish gut and acetone.

'OK, let's make it that!' he said with a smile.

He refused to answer any more questions. The reporters were ushered out as the photographers were taking one last series of pictures. Visibly relieved, they emerged into the fresh air where catering staff were offering sweeteners in the form of cold cuts and excellent vintage termite wine.

226 Maximulian Chun owned a mining empire. The firm was several million years old; it had belonged to the family ever since Aurora Mau, the original mother of the andropods, had panned out the first grain of gold from the kerosene slopes in the wild Yunni Mountains. From that sparkling beginning the operation expanded via small concessions, test mines, wells, veins of ore and pit-shafts to gigantic smelting plants and well-trained armies of miners who bought up and smelted down whole planets at a time.

The peak had been reached relatively recently. They had penetrated as far as the centre of the universe. In contrast to what had been thought previously, the universe was not chaotic. It was not an expanding porridge of galaxies hurled out here and there at random. The universe had a form. The form was so colossal in scale that, before now, it had not been possible to obtain an overall view of it, but it had a form nevertheless.

A disc, many of you will have guessed. A spiral, others might think. Or even something as simple as an expanding sphere.

Wrong, wrong, wrong. The universe takes the form of . . . stand by to be astounded. You're not going to believe me. You won't be able to grasp this properly.

A prick professor.

The universe actually looks like a prick professor. It's a most unfortunate fact, one would have wished for something more dignified. A spiral or a sphere, yes, I couldn't agree with you more. Even today, quite a lot of governments have refused to accept the truth. The leading scientists from several noted civilisations therefore decided, at a recent astronomy conference, that action must be taken. An information campaign must be launched. The taboo would have to be broken, we must start talking openly about the matter. Whenever possible they would keep hammering home the message, until it finally achieved universal acceptance. These were not street urchins, note, but modern cosmology's most dedicated supporters who answered every question on the questionnaire circulated throughout the universe with the words 'prick professor'.

Even worse was the fact that the absolute centre of the universe, in other words, its innermost point, schematically speaking, was the professor's sexual organ. Hence, a number of leading astronomers had worked out how to put their agitation to maximum effect and take it a stage further. Purely as part of an information campaign, they had resolved to use the word whenever possible:

'Dear Vice Chancellor, prick, I am writing in order to request an increase in research funding for the next budget year, prick.'

Yes, I know, tiresome in the long run. Before long, every wall on campus was covered in the professors' prick graffiti. The whole business soon got out of hand. Whenever public reaction didn't seem to respond quickly enough, in the interests of science, quite a lot of male cosmologists began taking out their willies while lecturing. They would stand by the overhead projector, swinging their penises from side to side and slapping them down rhythmically on the desk to help bring home the points they were making.

Anyway, Chun's mining engineers had got as far as the centre of the universe. As they approached they could see the colossal, gruesomely black hole hovering in front of them. Like the plug hole in a vast bath tub, it sucked into itself all the dirty water and compressed it until time and place ceased to exist.

The bathtub whirlpool comprised a galactic swarm of suns and planets, clouds of gas and dark matter swirling round and round at an ever-increasing speed. And it was the long drawn-out banana shape of this whirling helix that constituted the prick of the prick professor. The innermost layers were sucked into the hole in association with an explosive burst of energy, while the surrounding space was filled by new matter. In short, this was an ideal location for a mining company eager to acquire cheap, obsolescent planet systems. It was merely a question of grabbing hold of the heavenly bodies, extracting the best bits, and letting the rest be sucked into the hole. Shyupp, it said, as the planets were slaughtered in Maximulian Chun's gigantic smelting factory. Shyupp . . . shyupp . . . shyupp . . . Or rather, pling . . . pling . . . pling . . . in Mr Chun's bank deposit boxes.

As time went by, the prospecting operation came closer and closer to the very edge, the plughole leading down into the black hole. The precipitous, conical abyss out of which there was no turning back. The miners had tales to tell about sights that no eye in the universe had ever seen before. Just as the irresistible descent began, shortly before light itself was swallowed up by the hole, matter was stretched out by unstoppable gravitational forces. Planets were elongated until they became nothing more than an incredibly long line, like a rubber band being stretched more and more, as continents were reduced to rubble, stones were reduced to specks of dust, and eventually even molecules were torn apart by the cosmic forces. And the moment before everything disappeared, before matter was swallowed up by darkness, it transmitted a death glow. One final flame-spitting firework display, cobalt blue and copper and cinnabar and blood, a screech of colours just before everything was sucked down into the depths and vanished for ever.

This was the scenario that inspired Chun's engineers to construct the so-called bath foam process. What the mining engineers discovered was that as matter swirled down towards extinction, it divided up into layers – just like cream and skimmed milk in an old-fashioned separator. From elements weighing next to nothing to increasingly heavy substances, layer upon layer. What they were observing before their very eyes was nothing less than the world's biggest spin-dryer. Beryllium was sparkling away on the surface, while titanium glittered much further down. And even further down was a yellowish, buttery ring sinking slowly, ever so slowly down into the funnel – pure, glistening gold.

But how to get at it? The designers cobbled together a neutrino Howitzer, inspired by the deadly weapons used in the latest galactic war. They aimed it at the rim of gold and bombarded it for all they were worth. The ultra-thin neutrino beam hit the metal, making it foam and turn into a fluffy neutrino froth, much lighter than anything else around. Gravity lost its grip and, reminiscent of a glittering soufflé, an intestine made up of gilded soap bubbles, a fluffy gold froth rose up from the abyss in a long string and was easy to catch.

It's easy to picture the scene. Miners standing on the platform, wearing their zirconium-welded armoured overalls so as not to be decimated by the gravitational pull. The rig circles round the abyss, the miners chase after the golden froth as it is washed up onto the rim and they vacuum it up as if it were no more than a wisp of smoke. A valuable, dense perfume rising up out of the monster's bellowing throat. The tiniest mistake could be disastrous. Everybody remembers the technician who tripped and stumbled into the security barrier. He screamed in horror into his intercom as the seams of his armoured overalls split and he was rapidly stretched out to form what looked like a fishing line, a damp, red sewing thread.

You balance on the edge of the abyss. Circle like a pilot fish round the enormous, ravenous sucking force of the universe. The team wrestles with the controls, the golden froth floats into the collector, a red glow rises up from the blast furnaces at the heart of the rig, cargo shuttles come and go, supplying the bulging, black crude-metal freighters out there in the darkness. Everybody is on tenterhooks. They are working constantly at the limits of their capacity, gravity pulls and pushes at the reinforced welded joints, steel plates are shorn through, gaskets and pipes start to leak. Non-stop noise, warning lights, emergency call-outs with dosimeters and tool boxes, puffing and panting behind visors that repeatedly mist up. The smell of sweat and ozone, a metallic taste in the mouth.

In the midst of all this, a firefly suddenly appears. Deep down in the abyss. A tiny, fluttering spot of light that seems to be moving slowly upwards. It rises like the bubble in a tall champagne glass, apparently unaffected by the inferno on all sides.

The tiny spot starts to grow. At first it looks like a mosquito, then a fluttering dove. White and semi-transparent it swells up and becomes a Zeppelin, but with a much softer outline. Flimsy and amoeba-like it emerges from the maelstrom, comes closer. With a damp smack it eventually lands on the platform of the ore rig, quivering like a crème caramel. It must be about sixty metres long. You can just about make out segments. Hollows, blisters, liver-coloured organs.

The team stands there as if petrified. Some drop their tools. They've gone mad, mental illness has caught up with them. They're staring at a gob of spittle, as big as a block of flats.

The next moment membranes open up. Out through the cell wall come big larvae: fat, brownish sealsacks wriggling their way forward. They line up in front of the collector and its articulated jib, and are apparently trying to communicate with it. Only now do the rig workers come to life. They struggle to unhasp the container marked *Alien Life Forms*, and start the translator going, scanning the faint squeaks made by the sealsacks. Then they compare them with the millions of languages stored in its memory. No hits. So they try the most basic 'language' of all: Basic Binary Communication. The aliens pull a string of mucous membrane out of their spacecraft and attach it to the translator. After a lengthy exchange of data, the parties manage to find a primitive computer language that they can both decipher.

The first words come from the visitors. One brief sentence:

'Three in the den.'

The commander of the rig, who has stationed himself next to the translator, assumes that it's some kind of greeting.

'And good day to you,' he replies.

'You carbon.'

'Eh?'

'You are carbon.'

Then the penny drops.

'Yes, we are carbon-based creatures. Absolutely right. Carbon is what we are.'

'We neutrino.'

'You are made up of neutrinos?'

'Absolutely right. Neutrino what we are.'

The guests were apparently from a different universe. A neutrino universe whose entrance was somewhere down there in the infernal abyss. The black hole evidently acted as a kind of lens: if you entered into it using the right kind of spacecraft you could be reflected out on the other side, in one piece.

'What does your universe look like?' wondered the commander.

It was evidently not so easy to explain this, using

the primitive computer language. The range of vocabulary was not exactly ideal. But it was a place with a lot of advantages, that much was clear. There was no gravity there, for instance.

'No gravity?'

'No, punched cards. Punched cards better.'

Eeehh . . . ? A universe based on punched cards?

'Punched cards better,' they insisted. 'Punched cards stronger.'

OK, OK. Punched cards were terrific, we could see that with our own eyes. They had managed to produce intelligent snot, after all.

With a lot of humming and hawing and complicated flattery, the guests began to come out with what they really wanted. They were hoping to do business. It had to do with our black hole. They wanted to buy it.

'Buy the black hole?'

Yes, or a part of it, at least. As much as we could spare. They wanted to get at the plasma. The plasma porridge itself down there. How many zillion tonnes might we be able to consider selling?

The commander asked them to repeat their request. They did so. There followed a lengthy silence. In the end he asked them politely for time to think the matter over. The aliens promised to return, went back to their flimsy spacecraft and slithered back into the plughole.

The commander immediately sent an express message to Maximulian Chun. The problem was that Chun had just swallowed a handful of skinned beaver flesh and then taken an afternoon nap. When he eventually came round, he slid voluptuously into his swimming pool – and saw the company chairman running towards him with the telegram.

Sell a black hole? He'd done less attractive business than that before.

'Hmm,' said the chairman of the board. 'There's a complication. A little detail. Well, not all that little a detail, to be honest: a rather colossal detail.'

Out with it!

Maximulian Chun bobbed quietly up and down in his volcanic brew while his chairman spread out the diagrams. That particular black hole was a bit special. As was well-known, it was the biggest one in the universe. There was a risk that disturbing it could affect . . . the laws of nature.

And that was when Chun had his flash of genius. You know already what happened. He had the Intergalactic Institute of Public Opinion send out a questionnaire, then launched the biggest slimming campaign the world had ever seen and watched the cash tumbling into his bank account. Immediately after the stormy press conference with the indignant journalists, he put on his elastic-weave molybdenum kimono, as pliable as the finest silk. Then he boarded his wormhole yacht, felt the field of force being activated, and set off at express speed for the centre of the universe.

And so Maximulian Chun was on the spot when the sealsacks returned. They immediately started examining and negotiating the various proposals. But they found it difficult to reach agreement. In the end the guests produced something sticky and shiny. It was a neutrino costume, and after some hesitation Maximulian Chun put it on. Then he climbed aboard the flimsy spacecraft, slid slowly down into the black hole and was swallowed up. He would be the first creature in the history of the world to visit an alien universe.

The next morning the crew of the rig woke up in a strange, cheerful mood. They felt surprisingly full of beans. They were up the stairs and into the breakfast canteen in a jiffy. And when they sat down by the picture windows, they could hardly believe their eyes.

The black hole had shrunk. All the banana-shaped bathtub-whirlpool surrounding it had withered away.

All that remained of the original giant sexual organ was a modest little hole and an eddy sucking in ever so slowly a few cloudy gas planets. The form of the universe had changed. The prick professor had turned into a vagina professor.

And why did their bodies feel so strong, what had caused that? The cutlery felt too light, they were putting too much effort into holding the knives and forks. All over the canteen, the crew were spilling and dropping food, and laughing in embarrassment.

All over our gigantic universe, the same discovery was being made. Everybody woke up feeling strong. They started fumbling and breaking things. And eventually, almost as an afterthought, they went to their bathroom scales and weighed themselves. Stepped down. Checked the settings, then tried again.

It was a miracle. They had lost weight during the night.

In science laboratories, researchers were measuring, calculating, measuring again, and were eventually forced to accept the obvious. The gravitational constant had changed. Nobody understood how it had come about. But it had certainly changed. In sports arenas all over the universe, the coming weeks saw the most incredible new world records being set.

Unfortunately, Maximulian Chun never returned from his excursion. But there is no doubt that his galactose method delivered what it had promised.

From then on a kilo weighed only eight hundred and fifty grams.

Night Shift

The spaceship is asleep. I'm the only one on the flight deck. Roger, the second officer, has gone to lie down in the on-call cabin and has dozed off in front of a film. I'm all alone, at the very front of this colossal ore freighter. A little mosquito, caught in a fold of skin on the snout of a charging blue whale. And it's the mosquito that's doing the steering. Me, with only the uttermost tip of my finger touching the sensor stick. The whole of this gigantic, swollen body behind me does my bidding, goes in whatever direction I indicate.

The temperature lights signal a warning. We are entering a cloud of gas, one of those many dark-coloured veils that wriggle along between stellar systems. Friction heats up the shields at the front of the craft and they start glowing a shade of red. I enjoy the silent theatre being enacted on the other side of the windows, feel my cheeks flushing in the reflected light.

A rose colour you hardly ever come across in space, the mild glow from an old hotplate you've forgotten to switch off.

And then phut! A cascade of colours. Gleaming strips, rainbows, fizzing and swelling all round the flight deck. The nocturnal darkness of space has vanished; our craft is passing through a firework display. Cosmic dust. Tiny stones being crushed with horrific force as our monster freighter races on and on. The alarm light starts flashing, and I adjust the protectors. I feel stimulated, slightly intoxicated. It's the adrenaline. Despite the fact that I ought to feel completely calm. The big, dangerous asteroids give enough of an echo for our systems to take avoiding action in good time. But nonetheless, you never know. There's always one chance in a hundred thousand that something will slip through. And then things start getting broken, the sirens screech, and quick as a flash you need to put on your pressure suit, get outside and start making repairs.

It soon eases off. We're through it. The shields cool down gradually, the red glow fades away and soon space is black once more. I carry out the safety tests, all systems are intact. Scribble a note in the logbook. Stretch out my arms, fold my hands behind the back of my neck. Hear the door open.

'Was there a problem?'

Roger's tousled hair shows he's just woken up.

'A hail storm.'

'The alarm went off.'

'It was a two, at most. I logged it as a two, but I suspect it was only a one, in fact.'

He sits down, yawns, rubs at the corner of his eyes.

'It was pretty,' I say.

'Hmm?'

'Colours.'

Then we sit in silence. Have a cup of coffee. Feel drowsiness like a heavy weight at the back of our heads.

At this very moment, as dawn approaches, the radar signals an emergency. We both lean over the plotter.

'A rock?' Roger wonders.

'Dunno.'

'Let's get out of the way manually, it's probably just a lump of gravel.'

I run the analysis programme. It only takes a second, then the screen turns an angry green.

'Oh no, surely not,' Roger groans. 'Not at this time in the morning.'

I feel the same lack of enthusiasm as he does. Start braking hard as the dot on the screen grows bigger and bigger. Now you can see the outline. No longer any doubt. It's a spaceship. I call it over and over again, but there's no reply. Ominous.

'Let's just ignore it,' Roger says.

But I continue braking. It's our duty to investigate if something seems to be wrong, maybe they've hit trouble. I switch on the searchlights and examine the thing through the window.

'Is it from home?'

I nod. An old Venus shuttle, in total darkness. The stays and masts sticking out on all sides make it look like a dead dragonfly. I keep on calling, but there is no reply.

'Shall we wake the others up?' Roger wonders.

I shake my head, well aware of how annoyed they would be.

'Let's draw lots,' I suggest.

He finds some dice and we both throw. I lose. Resigned, I climb down to the air dock and put on my spacesuit. I wriggle into the service capsule. Lie on my stomach by the controls as the capsule closes. The suction hatch slides up in front of me. I feel dizzy as I watch space opening up, this dark, star-studded abyss. I press the control lever and shoot out into weightlessness. It feels like falling into a deep-sea grave. The capsule disconnects itself from the freighter, a little spool-shaped plankton slinking out of the fold in the blue whale's skin. I glide towards the stranger like a glittering torpedo. I cautiously manoeuvre my way between the shattered shields and broken stays and soon find their docking hatch. It's dented and scarred, impossible to open. It must have been hit by something heavy. I continue tentatively along the hull until I see an emergency lock. I wriggle out of the capsule and try to open it manually. Hang on tightly outside my shell, exposed and helpless. I'm relieved to feel the lock giving way and the hatch slides up. White flakes of something or other come cascading out. I measure the pressure inside the gaping hole. It's almost zero. It's too late; it seems to be all over.

'A ghost ship,' I shout to Roger.

'You reckon?'

'There's virtually no air left inside. I'll go in and check it out.'

Somebody has to go in and investigate, that's what the rules say. There might be somebody in the coma freezer who can still be saved. Everything is pitch black inside; I switch on my helmet lamp as I swim in. The whole ship feels like a grave. A thin layer of dust rises up in the corridors. It looks like soot. Has there been a fire?

I start by searching the sleeping quarters. Empty. A few items of dirty clothing float around obscenely in the weightlessness. Long stockings, an artificial leather belt, a stained bandage. They look like grotesque snakes in the lamplight.

Ready for anything, I investigate further. A few empty plastic packages bob up and down in the corridor like jellyfish. I catch one of them: used blood plasma. Feeling increasingly uneasy I enter the navigation room. It is filled with small objects whirling round and round in the darkness. Plastic rubbish of some kind or other. Or are they lumps of ice? I catch one and see how it sparkles and has sharp edges. Broken silicate glass. I now see that every single plasma screen has been smashed. Perhaps the spaceship was attacked by pirates? The detritus keeps tapping at my visor as I swim round, an unpleasant pattering noise. There is no trace of the crew, no logbook. They must have abandoned ship using the rescue capsule.

The emergency radio is still on transmit. I tap at the controls, but all the reserve power was used up long ago. Then I notice a length of cord tied to the desk chair. It leads to under the desk. I struggle awkwardly to get down to floor level. Aim my helmet lamp, then start back in shock. A grinning skull. A grey and dried-up tongue. They had a dog with them. Its frontal bone has been shattered by something hard, a hammer perhaps. I feel sick as I try to stand up and collect my thoughts.

'It's empty!' I pant into the radio.

'Are you sure?'

'I've searched everywhere.'

'OK, I read you. Return to base.'

Panting heavily I emerge into the corridor again, Take a wrong turning and end up in a cupboard. There is food left in boxes on shelves. Packets of powder. Dried stew with lemon, spaghetti Bolognese. I check the use-by date: over twenty years ago.

'Is this tub registered?' I ask.

'It's listed as scrapped. I've checked everywhere, it must have been sold on the black market. An old banger that nobody missed.'

'I can't find any crew.'

'Return to base. You're running out of oxygen, the warning light's on. Return to base, and we'll blow the thing up.'

I hurry back. It would be fatal to get lost in this maze of corridors. I came from that direction. But I've never seen that door before. I must be lost.

'Calm down!' Roger shouts. 'You're gasping for breath! You're panicking!'

I yank the door open. Out tumbles a spacesuit, so inflated by gas that it's threatening to burst. I can see a face behind the visor. The eyes are covered in green mould.

'Aaarrgh!' I cry.

'Return to base. Just get out of there. Return to base!'

'It's a girl,' I say, heaving. 'She's fermented.'

I take a pair of pliers out of my front pocket. Fumble for the girl's swollen glove, take hold of her thumb. Averting my face, I clip it off. The cloudy gases squirt out of the hole in the spacesuit with enormous force. The body is tossed about like a marionette, flailing and kicking with jointless limbs.

'Go backwards!' Roger yells. 'Backwards and then to your right.'

I scramble backwards and to the right. And come to the emergency lock.

'I hate this,' I whimper.

I return, exhausted, to the mother ship, shivering uncontrollably. We deep-freeze the thumb in accordance with regulations, for DNA identification. Then we use a satchel charge to blow up the ghost ship, transforming the whole coffin into a cloud of swirling cosmic dust.

All the time I can see the dog in my mind's eye. The

girl must have stroked its silky-smooth snout as the end approached, begging forgiveness. She would have gazed deep into those brown eyes while the dog's tail was slamming hopefully against the cabin floor. Time and time again she would have raised the hammer, but been forced to lower it again. Tried to convince herself that its suffering would be reduced. That she was doing what she had to do, out of love.

248   There had been a name on the dog's collar. She had called it Laika.

0.002

The most significant event in the history of the Earth happened to take place one Midsummer Eve in the northern Finnish town of Oulu. It was thanks mainly to the weather. That evening the whole of Europe was enveloped by a trough of low pressure, unusually dense for the time of year, and hence most of the continent was covered by grey, impenetrable clouds. Apart from the far north. The Finnish forests gleamed invitingly in the evening sun, the ten thousand lakes sparkled like jewels, and from villages and beaches smoke rose from the countless Finnish midsummer bonfires.

Just outside Oulu, on the shore of Lake Pyykösjärvi, the Finnish school caretaker Arto Liinanki was gnawing at a grilled sausage. The heat from the bonfire was turning his face red and grease from the sausage was dripping from his lips.

We ought to have some mustard, he thought. A pity I forgot the mustard.

Standing or sitting round the fire were about twenty other people; bottles of beer were sparkling in the grass, a woman in a denim jacket was hunched over a guitar, humming away.

'Has anybody got some mustard?' Arto shouted.

'In the boot of my car,' said Kimmo, pointing, and skilfully opened another bottle of beer with a cigarette lighter.

Arto marched off towards the car park, swaying slightly. A few mosquitoes whined doggedly around the back of his head. He passed by a copse of birch trees and paused to empty his bladder. He opened his zip with his free hand and aimed the warm jet at a white, almost silvery-white, birch trunk.

When he turned round they were standing there. Four of them. Tall and thin in lead-grey protective overalls.

His first reaction was a half laugh. Some youngsters dressing up. But when they simply carried on staring at him, he started to feel scared.

They're going to mug me, he thought. My watch, my mobile . . .

One of the creatures then raised its surprisingly

supple stork-leg in the direction of its head and opened its visor. You could see a beak inside there. It made pecking movements. It seemed to be tasting the air, making soft clicking sounds.

Hands trembling, Arto held out his half-eaten *lenkkimakkara*. The alien leaned forward and hesitantly picked up the sausage with the very tip of its beak.

'There's mustard in the car,' Arto whispered.

And these words, this simple sentence, thus passed into the history of the world. They were the first words that had ever been exchanged by a human being and an extra-terrestrial intelligence. There's mustard in the car. Spoken in the Finnish language, one sun-drenched Midsummer Eve by the northern Finnish lake Pyykösjärvi.

The shock waves spread over the whole planet. The whole of the Earth's crust seemed to start quaking under everybody's feet, and when humanity got up to face a new day, the news was trumpeted on every street corner:

'UFO in Finland! Space has landed!'

And underneath the headline a photograph of Arto gaping incredulously and saying:

'There's mustard in the car!'

During the course of the following day the world's press assembled at the Pyykösjärvi birch copse, behind the police barriers. The visitors' little conical landing craft could be seen on the lush grass. The president of Finland, a lady, had just partaken of her traditional Åland midsummer pike when the news reached her. Now she was standing here, having been whisked to Lake Pyykösjärvi by helicopter, delivering an official speech of welcome to the extra-terrestrials. Noticeably affected by the solemnity of the moment, she wished them peace and well-being. And then handed over a gift, a hand-carved *kantele*, a traditional Finnish zither; the visitors plucked at it bemusedly. Hundreds of television cameras buzzed away and the live broadcast reached all corners of the world. Behind the row of police officers the visitors began exploring the birch copse, taking samples of leaves and twigs and catching mosquitoes and caterpillars in metallic containers. Every now and then they would push up their visors, and then cameras would flash like lightning.

Before long the rumours were in full flow. The whole thing was a cleverly set-up bluff, of course. The visitors were just actors dressed up, and the spacecraft had been made in a Bulgarian film studio. Arto Liinanki helped to perpetrate the biggest practical joke of all time. Churches all over the world were prominent amongst those voicing their suspicions. There was nothing in the Bible about extra-terrestrials. The good Lord would never have created such monstrosities. That very same evening the Pentecostal pastor Juhani Peltola managed to force his way through the police cordon and rush up to the closest of the visitors. Peltola grabbed hold of the rubber mask and gave it a hard tug in an effort to pull it off but in a flash had his index finger bitten off by the creature's lightning-fast beak. The whole incident was replayed over and over again in news broadcasts all over the world, and the doubters fell silent.

By the very next day, the visitors had succeeded in writing a computer program to produce comprehensible Finnish, and hence were able to communicate by means of their portable data boxes.

'Where do you come from?' shouted the reporters. 'Who are you? What is your message for mankind?'

The visitors listened and calmly worked out what had been said. Then they explained that the questions had been asked too soon. They would make a statement all in good time.

During the following week the visitors taught themselves a few dozen more Earth languages. They started following all the planet's radio and television broadcasts, downloaded a few million web pages, and copied all the published material they could find about the scientific, ethnic and sociological development of the planet.

Then they called a press conference. It was time for their meticulously prepared statement. Their message for mankind. The announcement was brief, and comprised purely and simply:

'0.002.'

Nobody had the slightest idea what that meant. But the visitors persisted in repeating it: 0.002. That was the best they could offer. They had applied the cosmic standard test procedures that were universally acknowledged to be reliable and objective and if we earthlings were interested in becoming members of the cosmic parliament, then our vote would be worth 0.002 standard votes.

Two thousandths.

Their own civilisation had 385 standard votes. Calculated in accordance with the same objective test. If you are intelligent, you are intelligent. That's all there is to it.

There was an outcry. The United Nations called an emergency meeting. 0.002 was an insult! One planet, one vote. Otherwise you can stuff your cosmic parliament.

'You would go up to 0.003 if you stopped waging war,' was the response.

'Disgraceful! Undemocratic, it's ridiculous!'

'You're not worth more than 0.002. Can't you understand that? After all, you can't even read.'

'Of course we can read, what a lot of nonsense!'

'You can't even read anybody's thoughts. It's pathetic. You're at such a low level that even our fistular maggots are more developed than you are.'

'Fistular maggots! 0.002! Watch your tongues or we'll confiscate that space potty you came in and pickle you in formalin and put you on show.'

Zzoooom! They left. Soon afterwards it was realised that all the Earth's titanium mines had been emptied. The visitors had in fact been a gang of confidence tricksters who pretended to study us while their remote-controlled collection robots sneaked around and took all the titanium they could find back to the mother ship somewhere up there. We'd been hoodwinked.

The visitors disappeared into the galaxies and no doubt boasted in every galactic bar about how smart they had been. How they'd tricked the shirts off the backs of the natives. In that way the Earth's coordinates were spread all over space and it wasn't long before the next exotic visitors turned up. There were photos of cucumbers in the newspapers, violet-coloured stiff-haired cucumbers with grey suckers for feet, cucumbers whose behaviour and manners were so refined and urbane that we seemed like monkeys by comparison.

Monkeys. If only we could have been ranked so highly.

After an initial and totally understandable suspicion on the part of the earthlings, the cucumbers eventually managed to convince us that they were the genuine representatives of the cosmic parliament. They carried out their measurements and analyses diplomatically and came to the conclusion that 0.002 was too low a vote allocation for us earthlings. It ought to be 0.003. It was good, incidentally, that we had stopped waging war recently as that put us on a level with the fistular maggots back home.

When the cucumbers had left, anthropologists started visiting. Word had spread to universities and colleges all over the firmament. A new civilisation had been discovered and everybody wanted to be the first to describe us.

This process could be extremely irritating. Imagine sitting at home, watching sport on the telly. There's an exciting cup final on a cable channel, Liverpool v Juventus, and you've forecast a result 2–1 to Liverpool on your pools coupon. There are seven minutes to go, and it's 1–1. But Liverpool are attacking, the Juventus defender Scarlatti has been sent off and the home crowd is going wild with excitement.

Then a bluish sardine about ten centimetres long flops down onto your coffee table.

'Excuse me, what you doing?' it squeaks.

'Shut up,' you say.

'I no disturb,' it assures you. 'Just research what you doing.'

'Watching football.'

'Why you watching football?'

'It's exciting.'

'Exciting how?'

'Who's going to win.'

Liverpool are awarded a free kick just outside the penalty area. A curler going like a rocket, bounces back off the bar, mayhem in front of the Juventus goalkeeper, open goal, noooo . . .

'Why you said "noooo"?'

'They missed, dammit!'

'Missed with the white?'

'It's called the ball.'

'Are you sad now? You sad? You are it?'

'Shut up, for Chrissake!'

All is quiet for a while. Juventus counter-attack, a dangerous shot. A head in the way. Corner.

'What you drinking?'

'Beer.'

'It called beer?'

'Yep.'

'Can I take beer?'

You glance at the sardine. It gapes back with its pop-eyes.

'Nope,' you say.

'Please, just little.'

Short corner, quick passing move. The defence sweeps up. Counter-attack. You pour a drop of beer onto the table top to put a stop to the nagging. The fish wriggles over to it and fills a tiny pipette.

'What you have in hand?' it asks.

'Pools coupon, what else?'

'What it does?'

'I forecast the result of the match.'

'Why?'

'To win money.'

Silence again. Two minutes to go of normal time. Liverpool are attacking down the right wing.

'You win money?'

'If Liverpool score a goal, I'll win some money – now please put a bloody sock in it!'

It is actually silent. But only for a moment.

'So you not know how it go?'

'No, for Chrissake!'

'You no see in the future?'

'Afraid not!'

'You not know the black and whites make goal soon?'

'Juventus?'

'Soon.'

'Juventus score a goal? No, it's Liverpool who are piling on the pressure.'

'It is with the head, now it comes. You really no see in the future?'

At that very moment the Juventus goalkeeper pulls the ball out of the air and immediately punts it up into the centre circle. A fancy dribble down the right wing, a wicked cross, a header by Lodigliani . . . Goal! Juventus lead 2–1.

'With the head,' it squeaks. 'I said with the head.'

With a roar of disappointment you bang the beer

glass down on the coffee table. It sounds unexpectedly muffled, plosh. And as the referee blows the final whistle and the Juventus players form a writhing heap as they celebrate, the sardine lies there, squashed against the table.

'No! Sorry!' you yell. 'Chelsea–Barcelona? What's the result of the Chelsea–Barcelona match, please? This coming Wednesday?'

But it's already dead.

As time went by, of course, we earthlings also started travelling through the galaxies. We learned from the visitors the basics of antigravitation and wormhole navigation, and how to make super-strong spacecraft hulls from titanium composite. We were forced, of course, to buy the titanium at ridiculously inflated prices from space peddlers who happened to be passing. The first pioneering crew was made up of members from all parts of the world; time was up for the old racism. Out in space we would no longer be black, white, Jewish, aborigine. Simply humanoid. From the planet Earth, the Milky Way galaxy and our translation machines were programmed in advance:

'Greetings, strangers. Can we talk to your leader?'

When our first expedition returned several years

after leaving, the astronauts who clambered out of the spaceship were a grim-looking collection. The mass of journalists wondered excitedly if they had come into contact with other civilisations out there.

'Yes,' came the reply.

'But what did they say? What did they think of us? How did they rate us earthlings?'

The crew glanced furtively at one another. The chief technician cleared his throat but said nothing. The first mate and the chief engineer studied their toecaps. In the end it was the ship's doctor, a pale, elderly woman with very long fingers, who said very quietly what nobody wanted to hear:

'Fistular maggots.'

'What?' exclaimed the horde of journalists with one voice.

The crew members were ushered away to meet counsellors behind closed doors, where they were helped to recover from their traumatic experiences. Very little information leaked out, but a cleaner claimed that on one occasion he heard somebody inside there screaming so loudly that the walls vibrated:

'If only they'd called us monkeys at least!'

● ● ●

Space is hard. Space is ruthless. Space is an ice-cold mirror; it reveals everything, it shows things we want to forget, it conceals nothing, embellishes nothing, offers no comfort. And above all, space is abominably racist.

People would like to think otherwise. They have this image of democratic space crews from all corners of the universe with hairy lions as pilots, cheerful service robots and heroic humanoids who endure hardships in a spirit of wholehearted solidarity. You see that kind of thing in films sometimes.

But actually, it's extremely hard going. In fact, to be honest, it's insufferable. Everybody wants to be superior, to stand on top of the dunghill and look down on the plebs. And what is it that makes a civilisation superior? Well, that's the commonest topic of conversation at posh calligraphic dinners. Is it intelligence? Is it the intellectual level? Religiosity? Is it ethics? The ability to read the thoughts of others? The extremely refined table manners? Or perhaps the high age of the civilisation involved?

It was from these discussions that the cosmic test evolved. Agreement was reached on allocating marks objectively for the qualities of various civilisations and life forms. Several thousand points were listed, ranging from historical development and the presence of a written language to psychokinesis and the ability to use willpower to change the weather. The test was applied to all known civilisations, and those that came out on top eventually began to regard themselves as gods. And it's true that they had quite a few remarkable abilities, such as making bushes burst into flames or speaking in a voice of thunder, but there was no need to go over the top.

At the same time, they looked down on everybody else. And all the others followed suit and also started looking down on everybody else. The universe became increasingly a sort of mutual admiration society. The superior beings became so refined that they stopped having bowel movements. It was all A-list celebrities and platinum cards and VIP lanes, way above the heads of the masses. And this was the infernal class-ridden society into which our first expedition from the Earth intruded.

We ought to know a bit about fistular maggots as well. They live inside fistulas. More specifically, inside the arses of mammoth-like ruminants the size of skyscrapers. Blisters filled with fluid form inside their gigantic backsides, and the blisters are criss-crossed with blood vessels that suck up nourishment and energy from the host animal's large intestine and what passes through it. Inside the blisters, perfectly protected, up to a hundred or so good-natured parasitic maggots wriggle around, living off whatever the blisters suck up. The host animals can sometimes live to be eight hundred or even a thousand years old, so the maggots have plenty of time to sit around and think deep thoughts. Lots of philosophical discussions take place about this and that. An innate intellectual intelligence has been developed and increasingly refined over millions of years. And thanks to their exceptionally high intellectual mark, then, they achieved the same score as we earthlings in the cosmic test.

Unfortunately, jokes started spreading about earthlings:

'What do an earthling and a fistular maggot have in common?'

Answer: '0.002.'

Salvos of laughter make the crystal glass chandeliers rattle.

'What's the difference between a fistular maggot and an earthling?'

'One has its head in shit, the other has shit in its head.'

Even louder guffaws.

It was hard going at first, it certainly was. And it was hard going later as well. In fact, it's still hard going. But what can we do? Homo sapiens is among the dregs of the universe, and we're likely to stay there for a few more millions of years, given how slowly evolution takes place. We sit right at the very back of the cosmic parliament, and on the bench next to us are the fistular maggots. Right at the front are the superior civilisations, wallowing in the spotlights. They swagger up to the lectern and deliver brilliant speeches, long addresses of outstanding wit and erudition that are simplified step by step by the interpreters for the lesser civilisations, until they are reduced to the absolute basic level and tumble into our earphones:

'We consider that seven-dimensional writing should be used for the road signs along the Outer Ringroad. Seven-dimensional writing has advantages and we must keep abreast of the latest developments . . .'

Then comes the vote. We earthlings press the 'No' button and weigh in with our 0.002 votes (back to 0.002 because we've started waging war again). The fistular maggots do the same. The berk at the lectern presses the 'Yes' button and casts his 18,942 votes, and the superior civilisations win by a million yes votes to just over one-and-a-half no votes.

It's at moments like that you wish you were back in the wood sauna in Aareavaara.

Time's Last Angle

One evening at the beginning of September, maths teacher Öyvind Kuno was possessed by a spirit. He was in his summer cottage at the time, a red-painted wooden cabin near Strömsund in Jämtland, northern Sweden. He had just filled a bucketful of home-grown potatoes. He was overcome by a feeling of calm but intense happiness as he rubbed one of the newly lifted potatoes against his gardening glove to remove the skin, revealing the hard, yellowish white inside. Gingerly, he raised the fruit of the earth to his lips and took a bite. Then he chewed it. The taste of sweet starch filled his mouth, the taste of Jämtland's warm, steeply sloping summer. Perfection. Was there anything greater, anything more delightful than a crop of home-grown potatoes?

Öyvind bent down to grasp the handle of the galvanised bucket. His intention was to take the potatoes to the well, rinse them in the cold water, put them in a pan together with fresh dill and salt and simmer them gently in the evening glow. It was at that very moment, with his knees slightly bent, leaning forward and with one hand on the bucket handle, that Öyvind Kuno was possessed.

It came from the side. It hit him more or less side-on, and it hurt. Everything went blurry, then gradually returned to normal as the pain eased. Öyvind lifted up the bucket, his body functioned the same as usual. But he was no longer alone.

Later, when he had eaten his new potatoes with melted butter and schnapps and chilled beer and was sitting in front of the evening fire feeling slightly and pleasantly tipsy, it occurred to him that it might have been a micro-haemorrhage. A slight stroke in one of the small blood vessels of his brain. Something had burst and started to leak. But it ought to be all right again by now. No doubt everything was back to normal.

That was when it happened again. But slightly differently this time. A vague but nevertheless frightening feeling. It was as if somebody else had been trying to think, using his brain. Somebody else had taken up residence there.

He started reciting the exponential function of two – 4-8-16-32-64 – and got as far as 65,536 before taking a deep breath. He wasn't out of his mind. But perhaps he hadn't been cured either; that blood vessel might still be dripping into his brain making the pressure kept on rising so that when he woke up next morning, he would be paralysed beyond hope of a cure.

Only once before had he ever felt anything similar. That was when he was a student in Lund, and at the rag ball he'd tripped on acid. They had been in a cellar bar. He'd put the bit of paper into a glass of Val de Loire and emptied it in one gulp, still on a high from the excitement of the occasion. Somebody else had taken possession of him. A caramel-coloured stranger who was repainting inside his head. Öyvind had let it happen. Two of the revellers had started having sex on one of the bar sofas. Their bottoms were bouncing up and down like green phosphorus bombs, green juice was being sprayed left, right and centre. There was a smell of lemon and moist prick. But it passed over eventually, everything died away after a few hours. Turned grey.

I'll have another wee dram, Öyvind thought as he stood up from the armchair beside the open fire. A snifter to end all snifters!

He mixed the schnapps with a bottle of home-made blackcurrant juice he'd found in the cellar: made by the wife who had since left him. Blue-black blackcurrant juice, then lots of aquavit: the colour of the concoction in his glass turned ruby red, a veritable jewel. He felt sad when he remembered his wife. She had touched every one of those berries with the tips of her fingers.

The next morning he woke up on the crumpled kitchen mat with no memory of how he'd got there. When he looked around, he found that the furniture had been moved. Chairs were in the wrong place, the china cupboard door was open and four of the soup dishes were standing on the table. When he collected them in order to put them back where they belonged, he found that all of them contained potatoes. There were two in the first one. Four in the next. Then eight. And then sixteen.

Somebody had been using his body. While he was asleep. The booze, he thought. Perhaps it was just the booze. He put the potatoes back in the bucket. Then he shut his eyes. Just stood there, without moving, ears cocked, his hands resting on the substantial shelf of the drop-leaf table.

Then he said: 'Hello.'

Silence.

'Hello,' he said again. 'I know you're there.'

Then he saw a light in the corner of his eye. It looked like a collection of ethereal bubbles.

'What do you think you're doing?' whispered an angry voice. 'Why are you interfering in my life?'

The autumn term at the Wargentin School in Östersund was a difficult time for Öyvind. During the day he taught lethargic pupils about logarithmic functions and cubic equations, but as soon as he was alone he tried to get to know his inner stranger. It was not all that easy. The voice he heard wasn't really a voice, more of a perception. It came from the side, just like the bubbly light. If he turned his head to look at it, it vanished. The normal physical rules didn't apply to this phenomenon, you couldn't measure it or weigh it. Just listen with the outside of one shoulder. At right angles, as it were.

At first the stranger didn't want to give his name. But eventually he said his name was Ny-So. Or possibly Ni-Xå. Sometimes it sounded like Nilson. Annoyingly, Nilson maintained that it was Öyvind who had taken possession of him. It was Öyvind who ought to go away, not himself. Somehow or other they had got stuck to each other and now they couldn't get loose.

Given his scientific way of thinking, Öyvind suspected that he had become mentally ill. He had read descriptions of what happened. You started hearing voices, then you became afraid of radiation and taped aluminium foil over all your windows. Psychosis, he thought. Or stress. Perhaps I'm burnt out. He considered going to the doctor several times, but he would only refer him to a psychiatrist. He would be prescribed benzodiazepines. Or he might have to sit down and talk about his emotions, just like during the futile marriage counselling he had received when he and his wife split up.

'What are you feeling just now, Öyvind? Try to look your wife in the eye. She doesn't feel that you listen to what she says. She wants there to be real communication between the two of you, Öyvind.'

Nilson turned up at irregular intervals but as time went by Öyvind began to think he could detect a pattern. Nilson didn't normally appear in school, and almost never in the classrooms. But he did when Öyvind walked home. Or was in the shower. Or when he was watching the telly, slumped down in an armchair and feeling drowsy. It seemed that thoughts and activities kept Nilson away, but he made his presence felt the moment Öyvind relaxed.

It was on one such occasion that Öyvind decided that he'd had enough. He'd just eaten an excellent stew and was half asleep on his sofa-bed. His wife had taken the double bed because she had already started another relationship. With a radio journalist from Channel Four. No doubt he jabbered away all the time they were making love. She had wanted Öyvind to do that, wanted him to talk dirty: 'I'm going to screw you into the wall', stuff like that. Öyvind had been a bit shocked by it all. Or perhaps bashful. It was probably mainly bashfulness.

Now he was lying down and could feel the greasy, creamy stew spreading relaxation and sleepiness via his intestinal canal. And in the middle of the drowsiness Nilson started nagging:

'Go away,' said Nilson, over and over again. 'Go away, go away, go away . . .'

Öyvind yawned and closed his eyes. But the voice kept on:

'Get away from me, away from me, away from me, away from me, away from me, away from me, away from me, away from me . . .'

That was the moment when, disturbed on the threshold of slumber by this nerve-racking whining, that Öyvind really lost it.

'For fuck's sake shut your bloody trap!' he yelled.

It wasn't a yell made by his voice, but by his thoughts. Inwardly, into the darkness, as if he was using a powerful flashlight.

There was a shocked silence lasting for quite a while. Something inside there had been shaken.

'Excuse me?' it said eventually. As if uttered by a glow-worm, a little luminescent blip.

'Stop nagging me, Nilson. That's what I mean. For Chrissake, leave me in peace.'

'You leave me in peace.'

'You can have as much peace as you like, as long as you keep your trap shut.'

'You're the one who should keep your trap shut. All you think about every day is maths. Two four eight sixteen!'

'Of course. That's my work.'

'All I want is to get rid of you.'

'No, it's me who wants to get rid of you.'

'No, it's me who wants to get rid of you.'

'No, it's me who . . .'

At this point they both shut up. All of a sudden,

the whole situation seemed ridiculous. It was Nilson who took the first tentative step.

'We ought to talk this over.'

'Talk?' said Öyvind.

'Perhaps we ought to have real communication between the two of us.'

A brief silence.

'OK, you start,' said Öyvind, somewhat hesitantly. 'Say what you have to say. I'm listening.'

The next few weeks were the most remarkable and most bewildering that Öyvind Kuno had ever experienced. Every day when he came home from school he put down his briefcase, loosened his tie, unfastened the top button of his shirt, took off his glasses and lay down on the sofa-bed, eagerly awaiting what was to come. It took several minutes to shrug off the thoughts that had occupied his mind all day, to calm down. But then the moment came.

'Nilson,' he thought. 'Hi, Nilson, are you there?'

The conversation could last for hours on end. Towards evening he would get up, prepare something easy for dinner, sausage and mash perhaps. Then he would sit down and write out the conversation as he recalled it. Several notebooks were filled. Somewhat pretentiously, perhaps, Öyvind called them 'Parchments'. When he read them, he felt exuberant, even inspired. Or should he use an even stronger word? Should he dare to say *holy*?

As he wrote the parchments, Öyvind was finally convinced that Nilson really existed. His visions were not a result of some psychosis or a medieval obsession with hallucinations and stigmata. The fact was that Nilson existed and proved to be rational, even logical, in the way he thought.

'Nilson? Are you an angel?' Öyvind asked.

'Kindly define the concept of angel,' said Nilson.

Good thinking. First establish language. Then construct the world.

'Why do I only ever see you side-on, as it were, Nilson? I only ever get a sense of you out of the corner of my eye.'

'Come on, you are the one who's only visible from the corner of my eye.'

Öyvind thought that over for a while.

'An angel is a spiritual manifestation,' he explained. 'It can talk and think, but it doesn't comprise matter.'

'Then you must be an angel, Öyvind. That description fits you exactly.'

So, Nilson existed. But not in the way that we humans

understand the term. He wasn't really here and now. Perhaps 'angel' was a good word for that situation. Öyvind spent some time pondering the definition: he read Swedenborg's books of dreams; he studied Saint Birgitta's visions and revelations. And the more he read, the more convinced he became. They'd all been following the same track. He wasn't the first. Hildegard of Bingen. Job. Zarathustra. Giordano Bruno. Muhammad. Siddharta Gautama Buddha. They had all heard voices that they maintained came from a higher power. And all of them had changed the world.

But Öyvind Kuno was a scientist. No matter how much he was tempted, he couldn't submit to this. Angels or not angels, let that pass for the moment. Instead he took out a bundle of graph paper, and turned to his desk set of protractors, set-squares and French curves. Then he started drawing. He also contacted Nilson again, and asked a series of apparently innocent questions.

'Nilson, do you have a height? Yes, that's right: how tall are you? How wide? How much space do you occupy? Let us assume that you lie down in a bath filled up to the brim. Does any water spill out onto the floor?'

Nilson didn't understand the questions. No matter how much they explained and analysed their worlds, there was no common ground.

'But Nilson, let me put it like this. How long have we been talking together now?'

Nilson seemed to be thinking that over.

'How long?'

'Yes, precisely. How long, Nilson?'

'Hang on, let me think . . . Three angles, or thereabouts. Three.'

Öyvind checked his watch.

'Forty-five minutes. That seems to mean that an angle corresponds to fifteen minutes. Do you agree?'

'Yep,' said Nilson.

'Yesterday we talked for three and a half hours. That would be fourteen angles. Right?'

'Hang on, let me work it out . . . No, that's only two angles.'

'Fourteen, Nilson.'

'No, two and then another two. And now another two angles have passed.'

'But you said three only a minute ago.'

'I saw three from that angle. But I can only see two from here. Would you like me to go back and check?'

'Please do.'

Several minutes passed.

'Nilson? Nilson?'

'There's an angle getting in the way. That's why I can only see two from here.'

'Where the hell were you, Nilson? Just now?'

'I'm here all the time. But you didn't come, Öyvind.'

'You can't rewind time.'

'What do you mean?'

'I think we'll have to analyse this, Nilson.'

From Parchment 5:

Breakthrough. Nilson seems to exist as a sort of dinner plate. A disc that seems capable of rotating. He can rotate it at any moment. Hence, everything that has happened can be transformed to now. Now and now and now. From various angles. I think he is living in a different dimension from ours. Maybe the fifth, sixth, or seventh? The only dimension we seem to have in common is the fourth. Time. But time appears to be different in our two separate worlds.

Later in Parchment 5:

Nilson must live in a different universe from ours. He hasn't a clue about matter. We seem to see each other from the side, which is interesting. What if we belong to two different universes that glide through each other, like two streams of traffic at a crossroads? We just sense each other's presence out of the corners of our eyes. The traffic generally flows without any accidents and we pass through the crossroads without disturbing one another. But sometimes, very seldom, a human being moves in time at exactly the same spot as Nilson or his friends are moving in time, and so: Bang! We crash into each other. And then we can get stuck.

Parchment 6:

I asked Nilson to move forwards. Just half an angle or so. He said he was there already. So I closed my eyes and tried to make myself thoroughly empty. Had a strong perception of acidulous smells. Cucumber, cinnamon. I felt a sharp pain in my left ring finger. Unpleasant.

Parchment 6, the next morning:

That evening I had a visit from Ann Sejdemo, the stand-in philosophy teacher. She said she wanted to thank me for helping her with the attendance register. She brought with her an oriental salad and a bottle of wine. The salad smelled of cucumber and cinnamon. As I was opening the bottle of wine, I knocked a glass onto the floor. I picked up the shards and cut myself on my left ring finger, at the tip, where it hurts most. It's still throbbing. I'm in a daze. But not because of the pain. Nor because of Ann's gentle touch when she put a plaster on it for me. But because of the insight. Half an angle. I really think it works.

281

Over the next few weeks Öyvind repeated the experiment several times. On one occasion he managed to sense a powerful autumn storm that blew down a rotten birch tree which fell onto a neighbour's car parked in the street. Öyvind tried to persuade his neighbour to move the car before the storm arrived, but the man didn't realise how serious it was. The car roof was crushed, just as in Öyvind's vision.

Another time Öyvind saw how the school cleaner, Mrs Segerlind, a sullen Finland-Swedish woman with a smoker's cough and worn-down wooden clogs, was hit on the head by what looked like a lump of butter. The vision perplexed him. The lump was golden yellow with red stripes, and as big as a snowball; it hit her from diagonally above and caused her to fall headlong over her cleaning cart. In the course of a very confused conversation he urged her to protect her head for a while, by wearing a cycling helmet for instance. She glared at him and told him to go to hell.

About a month later she was diagnosed as having a brain tumour, already so advanced that it was incurable. She was put on sick leave immediately and never came back.

It was obvious. With Nilson's help Öyvind could see into the future. Time didn't move forward in a straight line; it was – like Nilson himself – similar to a dinner plate that you could turn round and round. Nilson could tramp around on it whenever he liked, while Öyvind clung onto his back, as it were. All he had to do was to keep his eyes open on the way. Some things were blurred, others clearer. Time was always the same, but the angle was new; the mountain peaks would drift apart, and new valleys became visible through the mist.

Parchment 7:

For human beings, time is an arrow. We have to follow the arrow forwards; all we see in front of us is the little cross made by the feathers, at eye level. Nilson, on the other hand, sees time from the side. The whole of his universe crosses ours from the side, and so from his point of view the path of the arrow looks like a length of string. Every human being has his own line, his own washing line with bits and bobs hanging from it. Thus millions of humans become millions of washing lines and side by side they form a sort of gigantic field with the whole lifespan of all humanity stretched out over it. A football pitch stuffed full with time. A bit like an Olympic Games opening ceremony when all the participating countries line up row upon row with their colourful national flags.

But the whole thing seems to be rather more complicated than that. A football pitch is rectangular, while Nilson seems to see time more as a circle, a vast LP. Time bends, the washing lines form spirals moving towards a denser and denser centre, and 'now' for a human being could be compared with the record player's feather-light stylus.

Hmm. He was straining a bit with his similes, poor old Öyvind. Arrow and stylus, washing lines and LPs. But the fact remained that now, whether he wanted to or not, he could make reliable predictions. One after another, his forecasts turned out to be correct. From the tiny little details to the more comprehensive prophecies. The only problem was the business of angles. He never managed to convert them into human clock-times and so he never knew exactly when his visions would turn into happenings. It might be tomorrow, or it could be next month. Or even some time several decades ahead. What he envisaged were not exact, photographic events, but were more like a rippling underwater landscape in character. They were a bit reminiscent of dreams, elusive. He tried to discuss it with Nilson:

'Has everything happened already, Nilson?'

'What exactly do you mean?'

'Is time already finished? Is its form fixed once and for all?'

'Yes.'

'But in that case we don't have free will, we are simply fulfilling our destinies, aren't we?'

'Of course we have free will.'

'But if everything is decided in advance . . .'

'You have your angles, old chap. You can wander about. You can't change time, but you can change the angles.'

'How?'

'By living, of course.'

'Hmm . . .'

'Don't sound so self-pitying.'

However, Nilson's advantage soon evened itself out in a most surprising way. One evening Öyvind was peeling potatoes outside his summer cottage, when he suddenly noticed that Nilson was watching him.

'Now I'll take the big potato,' Öyvind thought.

And so he peeled the big potato.

'Now I'll take that long one over there.'

And so he peeled the long one.

'Now I'm going to cut all the potatoes into thin slices with the kitchen knife.'

'Hu huu uuuh,' exclaimed Nilson, somewhere inside Öyvind's cerebral cortex.

'Now I shall melt a lump of butter in the frying pan.'

'It's melting!' yelled Nilson.

'Now I'll add the potato slices and it will start sizzling.'

'How . . . how did you know it was going to sizzle?'

'Now I'll stir it with the spatula,'

'Stop!' screamed Nilson. 'I'm going to faint!'

'Now I shall turn the potatoes and fry them on the other side.'

'Oo . . . hoooh . . .' spluttered Nilson.

'Hold your tongue while I'm eating, at least.'

'You know you're going to eat! You know you're going to eat! Now you're eating, you knew, you knew you were going to eat, aaaarrgh . . .'

'Nilson!'

Absolute silence. Nilson had flaked out. Öyvind never managed to work out precisely what had floored him, but it appeared to be something to do with our universe. Being able to do things in a certain order. For Nilson, that was the equivalent of taking a ladle of water and stretching it out to make a fishing line or an elastic and glittering spider's web.

'That's not on,' groaned Nilson as he came back to his senses. 'That's not possible . . .'

Öyvind chewed away at his potatoes without a word.

Parchment 8:

Prediction about the climate. It's going to get warmer. There'll be a shortage of snow in

Scandinavia. The ice linking the skerries in our arch-
ipelagos will become thinner and unreliable. The
oak tree will spread as far north as Östersund. Storks
and pelicans will start nesting in Värmland. I see
leeches. And then it will become cold, a white wall
of ice. People fleeing before advancing glaciers. I'm
not sure how long that will last. I see only milky
whiteness and frost from lots of different angles.

Prediction about politics. A grey woman will
emerge in Europe. Her lips resemble a whetted
knife. Concealed behind her are brothers, all
dressed alike. They claim to speak for the people.
They have a lot of money and are acquiring more
all the time. She has a child of steel who sparkles
when she lifts it up. The sky is filled with eyes.
A lot of birds circle around, their beaks eager to
strike. They land in England and are shot at.
Young people assemble in the streets. The woman
has a purse strung round her neck. Somebody
thrusts a tongue into her cleavage. She is badly
injured. A serious uprising ensues.

Prediction about illness. A great fever will
strike. It will cause deaths at airports and in
hotels. People will taste onions. Their blood will
thicken. Tumours will form, looking like bloated

bruises. Families will flee in panic. In hospitals, doctors will succumb to convulsions. Cities will be abandoned, the army will shoot at random. Cars will crash into roadblocks, trains will cease to operate. Queues miles long will form at barbed wire fences and in front of tanks. Hunger. Helicopters hovering. Priests wearing plastic protective overalls. Huge pits filled with fuel oil, bodies being thrown into the flames. Children staggering around, orphaned. The children fall ill, but survive. The youngest ones flourish. Something is happening to the world, colours are changing. Getting redder. A warm dawn, peaceful. Children's faces red. But there's a lot of work to do.

Öyvind sat in Ann's sun-drenched little two-roomed flat in Regementsgatan, high up, under the eaves. Everything was white, soaked in light. They drank sparkling tea by the open window as the curtains flapped gently in the breeze.

'I had to tell this to somebody,' said Öyvind as he drained his cup.

Ann was somewhat perplexed.

'Help me,' he pleaded.

She leaned forward and ran the tips of her finger-nails over the back of his hand.

'The world needs to know,' she said. 'You must say what you have to say.'

Inevitably, weighed down by fateful considerations, they ended up on her interior sprung mattress. She unbuttoned his shirt. Moistened the tips of her fingers, then rubbed them optimistically over his nipples. He lifted up her long summer skirt. She was wearing red silk panties. They were crotchless; he didn't need to pull them down.

Their first book, *Predictions*, was published by a one-man operation dedicated to New Age literature and launched on a seldom-visited website. It was hardly reviewed at all. Nobody at the Wargentin School in Östersund mentioned it and not even a third of the five hundred copies printed were sold.

But then came the great Greek earthquake. It was described on pages 75–78 of Öyvind's book, and among other things mentioned how the Parthenon would collapse and kill 'an athlete with damaged teeth'. One of the victims proved to be the Finnish ice hockey player and star of the NHL, Juhani Mäkinen, who had been among the tourists with the

Canadian ballet dancer he happened to be going out with at the time.

Several of the book's readers noted the similarities with Öyvind's description. *Predictions* received a positive review in the journal *Aura* and another hundred or so copies were sold. Nevertheless, not much attention was paid to the book – let's face it, an earthquake in Greece was the kind of prophecy that was bound to come true sooner or later.

And then heaven fell down on Jerusalem. It came hurtling down with a deafening shriek, smashed through the roof of a house and landed in a bedchamber where it massacred Israel's Minister of Defence who was fast asleep in his marriage bed. As if by a miracle, his wife survived more or less unscathed. Everybody thought at first that it was a terrorist attack, a shell fired by Hezbollah. But a few seconds beforehand, hundreds of people had seen a sparkling ball of fire in the night sky and it was soon established that it was in fact a meteorite.

In Öyvind's book, on pages 163–165, it states clearly that a stone will fall from the sky and kill a high-ranking Israeli soldier. This would be the beginning of peace negotiations that would lead to the foundation of a Palestinian state at last. Öyvind was right in that respect as well. God had hurled down punishment at the warrior prince, and thereby altered the course of history in true Old Testament fashion.

Over the next few years, *Predictions* sold four million copies. Foreign publishing houses bid astronomical sums for translation rights. Before long *Predictions* II and III appeared. In them Öyvind foresaw the velvet revolution in Pakistan, the malaria vaccine, the golf murderers, the USA's first black woman president, the abolition of celibacy for Roman Catholic priests, the extinction of the blue whale, alkaloid drugs, the reversing of the Earth's magnetism, the epidemic of childlessness in central Europe, the new volcanic island in the Gulf of Bothnia and the return of the sabre-toothed tiger.

The commotion raised was colossal. From all over the world came a constant stream of journalists, prophets, hippies, oracles, medicine men, ecstatics, and thousands of the merely curious. But Öyvind made himself unavailable. Ann explained that he was busy growing potatoes, making demanding inner journeys and writing what would be his final book of predictions. The one that would go further than any of the previous ones. The one that would go to the ultimate limit.

● ● ●

Predictions IV was given the subtitle 'Time's Last Angle'. They travelled there together, Öyvind and Nilson. Walked to the very edge of the pitch-black precipice. Now they are standing there, in silence. Down below them white seabirds are wheeling. Far, far down below the breakers are glittering, icy cold transparent foam. In front of them the history of the world comes to an end. Nothing but vast, windswept silence.

292   'There,' says Nilson, pointing and leaning out perilously far.

A rock jutting out. A jagged blue-black block of stone. You can just about see past it. Catch a glimpse of the ultimate, if you lean out far enough. They have arrived. At time's last angle.

And this is what will happen to the Earth. You are about to find out.

Gehenna. Yes, I'm afraid so. A big, devastating magma explosion. It comes from outside, from space, a gigantic heavenly body and all organic life burns up. The oceans boil dry and evaporate into space, the Earth becomes a barren, stone world.

But shortly before the end . . . Öyvind changes the angle slightly. Odd.

No matter how carefully he looks, Öyvind can find

no trace of human beings. Evidently they have already disappeared from the face of the Earth. Perhaps they were exterminated by a plague, or an atomic war. You can't see from this angle.

Instead, the Earth is ruled by ... dinosaurs! The dinosaurs have come back. They have developed higher intelligence and wander around in the autumn chill covered by some type of clothing. A metre-high race of velociraptors seems to have taken control; their craniums are swollen round unexpectedly large brains. They live in herds in quite large settlements and have developed astonishingly advanced solar energy technology with their little but very dexterous front extremities.

But humans? Not a trace. Dinosaur children can read about us in palaeontological textbooks. How once upon a time, a very long time ago, human beings ruled the world.

In the other direction along the precipice of time you can just about make out something even more grandiose. There you can actually see the end of the universe. The whole of space shrinks to form a snowball. A large, melting snowball, a lump becoming whiter and whiter and glittering with all the galaxies and nebulae, neutron stars and white dwarfs and all dust and invisible matter. The whole of our thinned-out universe is swept together like newly fallen snow outside your front door and bound together to form this giant lump, a colossal, melting ice cream that is being squeezed together to form plasma. All the stars and asteroids, all civilisations and black holes, everything, everything, everything is mashed together, absolutely everything – apart from one unremarkable little globule that slips out from between the fingers.

Eh?

No, what's going on?

One tiny little grain of sand slips through the fingers and disappears into the darkness. A successful attempt has been made to collect together all the matter in the entire universe, but one little speck has been missed! It runs away. It doesn't want to be annihilated. An unremarkable, tiny little grain that refuses to be melted down in the blazing oven, that makes a run for it, that hopes there might even now be a chance.

It's humanity. It's all the human beings who refuse to believe that this is the end. They have left the Earth in a bubble, a single shimmering spacecraft. They have learnt how to neutralise gravity. When the rest of the universe shrivels up to form a burning ball, human beings sneak out in the confusion. They carry on travelling. They refuse to give up hope. They stand huddled together in their shiny bubble, holding on to one another. In this beautiful little blue world, spinning round and round. Human beings don't want to die, that's why. Don't want to die. To disappear. They want to be there when everything starts all over again.

Ann sat on the patio of the summer cottage with the evening sun in her face. She was sipping something ruby red that Öyvind had concocted. Blackcurrant juice and vodka. It was like drinking the sun, the ball growing ever redder over the forests on the horizon.

Öyvind came out onto the patio with the potato casserole. Steaming new potatoes with sprigs of dill. The skin was as thin as leaves of silk. He spooned some carefully onto Ann's plate and dropped a lump of butter on top and watched it melt.

'The first ones this year,' he said. 'So tender, they send shivers down your spine.'

They ate as the evening breeze grew weaker and weaker and eventually everything was completely still. Like glass. Invisible, weightless glass. Ann took another sip of her drink.

'My wife picked the blackcurrants,' said Öyvind. 'There was a jar left in the cellar.'

Ann let the taste take possession of her. Felt her desire coming on. They would make love that evening.

'What's the situation with Nilson?' she wondered.

'Nilson's still there.'

'And what's he talking about?'

'You mean about what happened next? You think people will want to know?'

'Yes, what happened eventually to humanity?'

Öyvind gazed out over the forest, its floating still-ness. He stood up slowly and took a few hesitant steps onto the grass. Turned his head to one side, almost ninety degrees. Then he opened his eyes wide, his nostrils expanded as if in extreme terror. At that very moment the back of his head twitched, as if some-body had given him a hefty punch, an invisible pres-sure wave. He was thrown headlong to the ground. Blood poured out of his nose and ears.

'Öyvind!' screamed Ann and rushed over to him. 'Öyvind, say something!'

'Two,' he whispered. 'Four, eight, sixteen . . .'

His mouth felt warm. The back of his head was tingling. But Nilson had vanished. Öyvind could sense it straight away. They had been torn apart.

He sat up with difficulty. He was in considerable pain. Ann put her hands round his neck, bent down close to him and gazed in astonishment into his dilated, mirror-black pupils.

And she realised that it was over. The story was finished. We would never know.